Rosie Little's

CAUTIONARY
TALES FOR GIRLS

BY DANIELLE WOOD

MACADAM CAGE

Rosie Little's

CAUTIONARY
TALES FOR GIRLS

BY DANIELLE WOOD

For Xanthe (when she is older)
and in honour of
Saint Heather of the Immaculate Suitcase

Contents

Not for Good Girls

These are not, I should say from the outset, tales written for the benefit of good and well-behaved girls who always stick to the path when they go to Grandma's. Skipping along in their gingham frills — basket of scones, jam and clotted cream upon their arms — what need can these girls have for caution? Rather, these are tales for girls who have boots as stout as their hearts, and who are prepared to firmly lace them up (boots and hearts both) and step out into the wilds in search of what they desire. And since it cannot be expected that stout-booted, stout-hearted girls will grow up without misfortune or miscalculation of some kind, they require a reminder, from time to time, about the dangers that lurk both in dark forests and in the crevices of one's own imaginings. —*Rosie Little*

VIRGINITY

The Deflowering of Rosie Little

The trouble with *fellatio*, in my view, is its lack of onomatopoeia. Take more honest words like *suck*, or *gargle*, or *gurgle* and…ta-da! Their meanings are all neatly wrapped up in the way they sound. Whereas *fellatio*, all on its own, could leave you clueless. Especially in the week before your fifteenth birthday.

Fellatio could lead the uninitiated to envisage something ornate, baroque even — perhaps some sort of decorative globe, or a wrought-iron birdcage encrusted with stiff black vine leaves. Placed in a sentence: 'What a lovely *fellatio* you have on the sideboard, Mrs Hyphen-Wilson!'. Not, of course, that I had the opportunity to make such a mistake. Because although Cécile Volanges got Latin terms on the occasion of her deflowering, I, Rosie Little, did not.

I witnessed the seduction of Cécile Volanges more than once in the year I turned fifteen. Nightly for three weeks, the actor playing le Vicomte de Valmont in the local repertory theatre company's production of *Les Liaisons dangereuses* whispered to the ingenue Cécile — with the utmost delicacy, and from within the chintzy confines of a four-poster bed — *I think we might begin with one or two Latin terms.* And nightly for three weeks, I suspended my disbelief, more than willingly, endowing the set's plywood four-poster with all the solidity of pre-Revolutionary French oak, and thoughtfully touching up the dark stripe which, with each performance, was becoming incrementally more obvious in the parting of Cécile's yellow hair.

Le Vicomte would whisper and Cécile would squeal with pleasure and toss her blonde curls as she yielded into the softness of huge white pillows. And from various dark corners of the theatre auditorium I would watch, rapt, a stack of unsold programs just inches from my beating heart. I wanted desperately to hear the words that le Vicomte was about to trickle into the innocent ear of young Cécile. But each night, just as these spellbinding incantations of seduction were to be disclosed to me, the scene would fade to black.

So, although I ripped tickets and sold programs, *gratis*, for the entire season of *Les Liaisons dangereuses*, I did not learn the word *fellatio*. Neither did I learn the two neat, clipped syllables of *coitus* (a demure game played upon the decks of ocean liners?). And now, some years later and knowing one or two things more than I did in the week before my fifteenth birthday, I strongly suspect that even if my own seducer's vocabulary had stretched to *cunnilingus*, he would not have been terribly interested in its application.

In another country, in another time, a young man as well-off as Gerard Hyphen-Wilson (as I like to call him) would certainly have been schooled in Latin. His red-necked father would, with a little of his pocket change, have engaged a governess. Solemn of face and solemn of frock, she would have led him briskly through his first verbs. And later the little thug would have been sent away to boarding school, where he would learn to recite his Virgil, and perhaps utilise a few elementary Latin terms in his dealings with younger boys.

But not being in another country, or another time, Gerard Hyphen-Wilson had no Latin. In fact, the most interesting word I learned from the young lord of the manor was *snatch*. Placed in a sentence: 'Christ, your fucking *snatch* is tight'. For such was his eloquence as he clumsily ruptured my hymen while I lay beneath him on the splintery bed of a jetty in one of the better riverside suburbs.

I found myself in this rather unenviable, Latin-less position because my friend Eve had a boyfriend at Grammar, the exclusive boarding school that purported to educate all the thick-wristed, thick-witted farm boys within a 700-kilometre radius of our provincial centre. It was at a party to which we were invited by this prematurely shadow-jawed boyfriend that my deflowering was to occur.

Eve's father was an artist, which is no doubt why she knew Greek words like *phallic* and was able to deploy them, casually, in conversation. The time she described a rosebud in my mother's garden as 'a bit phallic' wasn't the first time I had heard her use the expression, or the first time that I had nodded and giggled, pretending I knew what she meant. But it was the time that compelled me to seek out the dictionary, from which I came away no wiser, since I had been searching under F.

I loved the painterly chaos of Eve's father's home, and the hippie-chic disorder of her mother's, every bit as much as she loved the fluffy white towels, hospital corners and tidy nuclear unit of mine. I scrambled to keep up with her, trying to learn the adult words that she knew, trying to match the distance that she would go with boys. But always, I found myself five steps behind. Even her body was ahead of mine, morphing into a desirable and womanly shape while mine remained painfully open to my father's taunt that you wouldn't see it past a matchstick with all the wood scraped off it.

The physical differences between Eve and myself were duly noted by a classmate of ours, Geoffrey Smethurst, who sat with us at lunchtimes when the other boys played handball, and who unkindly repeated to me a suggestion from one of the bitchier girls that I would be a wonderful presidential candidate for the Itty Bitty Titty Committee. Geoffrey was thin, with boofy black hair and a habit of doodling with biro on his forearms. His eyes fixed on the mounds in Eve's school jumper, he would remind us almost daily that all his out-of-school friends called him Skywalker, not Geoffrey. Still, I have him to thank for my early understanding of such important words as *prostitute*, *masturbate* and *franger*.

One day, when we had both sidled out of some kind of sporting activity and were alone together in a classroom, he waggled a finger of one hand and the thumb of the other at me.

'What would you prefer, do you reckon, long and thin, or short and fat?'

Frankly I thought both sounded rather revolting and wondered if it were necessary to choose, or if there was such a thing as a happy medium.

A Word from Rosie Little
ON PENISES

In the 1940s, Lieutenant William Schonfield made the important decision that it wasn't worth measuring flaccid penises. Their size, he reasoned, could fluctuate due to temperature and other factors so, *semper sursum*, Lt Schonfield took to the streets of New York and measured only the erect penises of 1500 men and boys. He discovered not only that the mean adult length was 15 centimetres, but also that more than 90 per cent of the penises he measured were over 11 centimetres long, and less than 5 per cent of them were shorter than 5.5 centimetres. Other research records the average length of a flaccid penis at 9.25 centimetres with a diameter of 3.125 centimetres, and the average length of an erect penis at 12.75 centimetres with a diameter of 4 centimetres.

It's also interesting to note that penises come in a marvellous array of shapes. A pig's penis, for example, mimics his corkscrew tail and can do the twist for more than 40 centimetres. (But surely this begs the question: what happens if a boy pig with a right-hand thread meets a girl pig who screws the other way?) Should you find a page of diagrams of primate penises, you could be forgiven for thinking you had glimpsed a page of designs by Gaudi for elaborate and protruberant roof details. A snake's penis splits in two at the end, rather like his forked tongue, and a tapir's penis resembles an anvil. The penises of cats and dogs have spines — possibly for the purpose of removing the coagulated semen of other males who got there first. And certain varieties of skate go extremely well equipped, having two penises to choose from on any given day.

Rumour has it that the band 10cc settled on its name because the average male ejaculation measured 9 cubic centimetres, and the band's members thought they could go one better. But the cubic centimetre is directly equivalent to the millilitre, and most research puts the average amount of discharge at between 3 millilitres and 5 millilitres. So if the 10cc christening story is true (which its members coyly deny), then the boys really were supremely confident about their capacity. One book thoughtfully measures out the average amount of discharge at between half and one teaspoon, just in case you were planning to cook with it. And those watching their weight should remember that there are 5 calories per teaspoon.

*

But on that day in the classroom, as I pondered the options so appealingly put forward by Geoffrey Smethurst, I knew none of this. (Neither did I know whether, when it happened, it would be okay to leave my top on to hide my embarrassingly small breasts. It seemed to me, from all the available evidence, that people mostly did it in the nude. But I wasn't certain that there was a prerequisite for breasts to be bared. After all, breasts weren't involved in the *actual mechanics* as far as I could tell.) And so it was that I found myself inadequately prepared for my first glimpse of a lavender-headed erection poking out of Gerard Hyphen-Wilson's pants.

The party to which Eve's boyfriend invited us was held in a boatshed owned by the Hyphen-Wilsons, which sat at the far end of a jetty, and which Mr Hyphen-Wilson Snr might have visited once or twice a year when he came down from the family seat. Whether young Gerard had come to possess the key by way of his father's blessing or his ignorance, I cannot say. I can say, definitively, that my parents had not sanctioned my attendance at this particular party. To the best of their knowledge, Eve and I were out watching a teen movie and putting in our mouths nothing more harmful than Minties and popcorn.

A pair of kerosene lanterns lit the interior of the boatshed, and in their tarnished glow I could see a dinghy hoisted into the rafters alongside some scrape-bottomed kayaks. I could make out oars propped against the bracing on timber walls and, nailed to a corkboard, a calendar. Although it was December, the calendar showed Miss August, who wore only the bottom half of a polka-dot bikini. She had tanned breasts with heavy brown nipples and glossy lips that were — almost needless to say — slightly parted. To the right of the calendar was the door to a rudimentary bunkhouse, behind which, by way of a small lapse of sisterhood, was Eve with her boyfriend.

The air was full of cigarette smoke and pheromones, both of which were rising in clouds off the dozen or so Grammar boarders who swung on fold-up chairs, or sprawled on the slatted floor, flicking their fag-ash through the gaps. I leaned against the splintery wall in my angora cardigan, concocting a demeanour that was at once frosty, challenging and flippant. (You might, equally, picture the boarders as a pack of eager and salivating hyenas, and me as the neatly trussed carcass of a small bird — a spatchcock, or possibly even a quail — dangling from the ceiling by a slender thread.)

'Drink?'

This, then, was the host — the leader of the pack. He had eyes that competed with each other to be closer to the bridge of his nose, and longish hair that made curling spaniel ears on either side of his face.

'Thank you.' I was polite, as you can see.

'A cocktail?'

'Sure.' And experienced, too.

'We only do one cocktail here,' said Gerard, making the others laugh.

'We call it the Rene Pogel,' said one of the laughers, rolling the 'r'.

Gerard ripped the ring-pull from a can of beer and took a long lug. Then he topped the can up with a greenish liquid from a square-cut bottle. When he passed it to me, it smelled minty and beery together.

'Crème de menthe,' he explained.

What was required, I decided, was a declaration of non-prissiness. And so I downed the contents of the can in three swallows and wiped my mouth with the back of my hand.

'Whoo-hoo! I think little Rosie likes our mate Rene,' said Gerard. 'Another?'

'Sure.'

Which went down the same way, leading to cheers and whistles. Things were going quite well, I thought.

'You don't get it, do you?'

He was very close to me now, fag-breath in my face.

'Get what?'

'Rene Pogel?'

'So?'

'Can you spell?'

'Of course I can spell.'

'But not backwards?'

Backwards? Oh. Oh shit.

It is worth mentioning, just in passing, that some men do not progress, in the evolutionary stakes, much beyond the proto-mentality of the Grammar boarders I met at the Hyphen-Wilson jetty that night. Only recently I encountered a man of forty who had amused himself by naming his — admittedly very swanky — yacht the Rene Pogel. But on the night I first became acquainted with this charming little ananym, Gerard watched me and waited and then, when he considered me sufficiently primed, led me through the door of the boatshed to the open decking beyond. After some alarmingly vigorous sucking at my mouth, he pulled me down onto the boards. Looking up I saw the moon, but it appeared to have turned its face the other way. I could hear the old ferry thumping out a bass heartbeat as she patrolled the estuary as part of her Friday night booze cruise. Closer was the rapid breathing of Gerard Hyphen-Wilson, whose great clumsy paws were up under my skirt and clumsily tugging at my tights. Soon I felt something hard and blunt butting between my legs, looking for a hole that didn't appear to be there.

'Christ, your fucking snatch is tight!'

I looked down to the opening in his fly, and understood that when my mother had told me about sex, she had omitted a rather important fact.

*

My mother is a nurse and she most emphatically does not believe in the use of silly words for body parts. She has this much in common with le Vicomte de Valmont, who advised young Cécile that in lovemaking, as in every science, it was important to call things by their proper names. In Sister Pat Little's view, 'wee-wee' is the most idiotic of the euphemisms for vagina, and when I was a child I was expressly forbidden to use it. Her insistence on correct anatomical terms was to have repercussions for the elderly groundsman at our school who didn't know where to look when I, aged five and dressed in my kindergarten smock, informed him that I had fallen over and hurt my vagina.

I recall stopping off once during a long drive, at a set of public conveniences on the side of the highway. The women's toilet block was full of the sound of trickling streams against metal and the wailing of a small girl who was making it known, between wails, that it hurt 'down there'.

'Does Aunt Mary hurt, darling?' asked an older woman, prim tones hushed.

'For God's sake — it's called a VAGINA!' my mother called out from within the safe confines of her cubicle. She would never have been so confrontational at the basin, I am certain.

Sex education occurred so early in the Little household that I have no clear recollection of it. To my mother, sexual intercourse was a fact, a bodily thing just like eating or having bowel movements. So secure was I in the knowledge that the penis went into the vagina that I had never stopped to wonder how, precisely. I had been exposed to a small range of floppy penises (not willies, not doodles, not dicks, but penises) in the course of a normal childhood. I'd had baths with my brother and seen his little bald worm of a penis. I'd seen my dad's larger and woollier arrangement. I'd even seen my grandfather's penis hanging over his big baggy sac. But that night, on a jetty in one of the better riverside suburbs, I encountered a penis doing something I had never seen a penis do before. It was sticking straight up, and its underside was all covered in veins. (Later, I would find my mother's sex education to be inadequate in the face of sperm as well. She had told me that it was a 'white, sticky substance'. Well, toothpaste is a white, sticky substance, and while I didn't exactly expect semen to come in various permutations of mint flavouring, I was surprised when it turned out to be an egg-whitish sort of muck.)

No four-poster bed, no chintzy curtains, no Vicomte slithering Latin delicacies into my ear. Instead, I was being deflowered by a jumble of Gerard Hyphen-Wilson's fingers and his sticky-up penis, one or the other or some combination of which caused a sudden splitting pain that made me squeal and pull at a hank of his hair in fury.

'Bitch!' he yelled. On top of me, he was red in the face and one of his pimples had burst, sending a little river of pus down one cheek.

'It's no good anyway, you're too fucking tight,' he complained, rolling off.

He manoeuvred my sluggish body until I was sitting

alongside him on the side of the jetty. I remember watching one of my patent leather pumps falling off my foot and floating away on the current, and the wobbly sensation that I was about to follow it. But then, Gerard's fat fingers were pressing small indentations into my scalp, and his purple-faced penis was just centimetres from my nose.

'So, what are you like at giving head?' he asked. As I said, Gerard Hyphen-Wilson had no Latin.

I now wish that I'd had the prescience to answer: 'Well, since I'm fourteen and I've never even heard the expression "giving head" before, let's just assume I'm fairly crap at it, whatever it is.' My response at the time, however, was significantly less articulate, being more of a gurgling sound in the back of my throat. Gerard was pushing my face towards his penis. What did he want to do? Stick it up my nose?

It was at this point that intervention came from a most unexpected source: Rene Pogel himself. Master Hyphen-Wilson thought he had Monsieur Pogel firmly on his side, but there can be too much Rene for a small-framed girl. My dinner of lobster thermidor and trifle, marinated in a frothy green soup of crème de menthe and beer, erupted from my mouth to cover the straining penis of Gerard Hyphen-Wilson, which was, suddenly, not straining so hard.

Of course it is easy to snigger, these years later, at that shrivelling penis coated in masticated seafood and liquor. But at the time, as Gerard Hyphen-Wilson's school mates scrambled out of the boatshed to see what all the shouting was about, I was hardly a picture of ha-ha, so-there composure. While he jumped about like an angry puppy, brushing the muck off his thighs, whining, 'Slag! The fucking little slag spewed on me', I was still flat on the boards emptying my stomach in small, violent bursts that clouded the water below. And this was the glorious image of my defloration that I was left to ponder the next day and for the long, long remainder of my high school career.

I wish you could see the various issues of teen magazines containing warm and euphemistic be-friends-first, always-wear-a-condom, it-might-hurt-a-teensy-bit accounts of the ideal first fuck, whose margins I filled with the ananymatic insults I might hurl at Master Hyphen-Wilson the next time I had the displeasure to see his leery face. *Elohesra!* and *Reknaw!* and *Trevrep!* I scribbled. Impotently, as it turned out. For I simply continued on my way — my basket lighter by one cherry — and never crossed his path again.

TRUTH

Elephantiasis

ELEPHANTIASIS

A chronic form of filariasis, due to lymphatic obstruction, characterised by enormous enlargement of the parts affected

—*Macquarie Dictionary*

My cousin Meredith has elephantiasis. To say this is not to imply that she is fat, though, coincidentally, she is. Not just a little overweight, but quite fat. Meredith has the kind of body that means shopping for clothes in the Big is Beautiful section; that entails judging carefully the width of chairs with arms. Hers is the kind of flesh that feels, sliding over it in supermarkets, in doctors' waiting rooms or worse, the Family Planning Clinic, the averting glances of whip-thin girls with blonde ponytails and long necks with which to flick them.

It's not only Meredith that has elephantiasis. Her villa unit — one of a set of brick and tile triplets nestled on a landscaped block — has elephantiasis also. In the lounge room, the suite is piled with plump cushions embroidered, cross-stitched, latch-hooked, printed and painted with elephants. Others are simply in the shape of elephants. Sentinel to the hearth are two mahogany elephants, which, by virtue of timber that is unrefined and almost hairy, bears a family resemblance to their ancestor, the woolly mammoth. The mantelpiece holds a passing parade of jade, serpentine, onyx, ebony and marble elephants. Elephants have even made it into the bathroom, where the plastic bodies of Babar and Celeste are filled with bubble bath. In the kitchen, the fridge door flutters with no fewer than six fliers (the one that arrived by chance in Meredith's own post augmented by five others passed on by thoughtful friends), all seeking donations to help an unfortunate Thai elephant, the victim of a landmine explosion, in need of a prosthetic foot. Each of the fliers is attached to the fridge with a separate elephant-shaped fridge magnet.

Meredith wonders at how quickly the elephant effect gained momentum. The first elephant, a palm-sized figurine carved in ivory-pale wood, was from no-one of particular consequence. The giver had sat next to Meredith in a personal development seminar, perhaps five years ago. She was a woman with raspy greying hair and a long crooked body which she was always shifting in her chair, as if simply sitting caused her pain in her bones. The woman mentioned she was planning a holiday to Africa, and Meredith — outside in the car park after the seminar was over — gave her a blow-up neck pillow for the plane journey. Meredith had found the pillow uncomfortable, and so it had been lying, deflated, in the boot of her car for months.

The second elephant was a soft toy, pale grey and plush. It

was also a thankyou gift, this time from a neighbour whose plumes of agapanthus Meredith watered while the neighbour was away nursing her sick mother. To this day Meredith does not know whether the neighbour chose the soft toy in response to the wooden African elephant on the (then relatively uncluttered) mantelpiece, or whether it was a purely coincidental choice. In any case, after that the elephantiasis spread like a virus to birthdays and Christmases, even to Easter, as friends, family and colleagues were seized by the thematic simplicity of it all.

> WHITE ELEPHANT
> An annoyingly useless possession
> —*Macquarie Dictionary*

The truth is that Meredith does not even like elephants, and never did particularly. Before they took over her life, Meredith had for elephants no special feelings. Now that the elephantiasis is advanced, her house a shrine to the order Proboscidea, she resents them. Perhaps, she thinks sometimes, the elephantiasis was a punishment for an act of bad faith: giving away a travel pillow that she already knew to be uncomfortable. She feels, however, that the punishment has gone far enough, since it is now her entire existence that is stretched out of shape, swollen up and distorted with elephants.

Could she have halted the stampede? Yes, almost certainly. She could, at some point, have mentioned that she would prefer to collect butterflies. Or springboks. In her most soul-bare moments she knows why she did not, does not. And it's not only because she is naturally conciliatory, and polite in a style that is grateful for a gift, no matter how awful. It's because she knows that her friends, family and colleagues see this (imagined) fondness of hers for elephants as proof of her jolliness. It is evidence of her good-natured acceptance of her fatness. A huge joke against herself. There she is, an elephantine woman surrounding herself with familiars. And a jolly fat woman without jolliness is left, she understands, with only one adjective.

A Word from Rosie Little
ON TOTEMIC WORSHIP

Gift shops thrive on people who have chosen — or, as in the case of Meredith, have had chosen for them — an animal totem. Perhaps it is a desire of the domesticated human to connect with an inner wildness that makes African safari animals such popular choices. Giraffes, lions and elephants are usually available as small carved wooden idols, keyrings, pencil cases with zippers down their backs, erasers, blown-glass trinkets and stuffed toys. Elephants, considered lucky, are more likely than the others to be found as tiny silver charms for a bracelet, tinkling against hearts, four-leaf clovers, horseshoes, money bags, and wishbones.

The Howards, who reside at Castle Howard of *Brideshead Revisited* fame, collect hippopotamuses. I once saw the hippos displayed in the castle's entrance portico, a frippery amid the ancient Greek statues, the overarching frescos, the great, heavy gilt of it all. In a glass cabinet are comic china hippopotamuses decked out for golfing, an elaborate Fabergé hippopotamus, and a group of serene grazing hippopotamuses etched into glass by a leading London artisan. Some of the hippopotamuses were given by the Howards to one another as anniversary gifts, while others have come from well-wishers who know the couple's proclivity for the animals and have no doubt thought of the couple when they've stumbled across an unusual one. The Howards are pleased to say that one of their favourite hippos — a wooden carving with large ears — was purchased for one pound and fifty pence at an Oxfam store. But they regret that they cannot have on display, due to its limited shelf-life, the charming carved-potato hippopotamus that was once sent to them by an admirer.

*

THE MEMORY OF AN ELEPHANT

—proverbial saying

*

For Meredith, the single worst thing about being a primary schoolteacher is the last day of the school year. On that day the children arrive, all glowing with the joy of giving, presents for teacher in hand. Even the grottiest boys are coy and sweet with gift-wrapped anticipation. Among the presents Meredith receives there is always a mug with an elephant's trunk as its handle. Some of these mugs are slip-cast with Dumbo-type elephants that have fat, pale-grey curves and pink inner ears. Others are of bone china, and bear more serious elephants with trunks finely ridged and delicate pale slivers for tusks. Usually, too, there is a cushion cover, lately in Indian-sari style with small circular mirrors blanket-stitched to the elephants' pink and orange saddles.

Meredith teaches at a private school, and there are newly moneyed parents who like to make expansive gestures of their gratitude. As a result her courtyard water feature (placed according to feng shui principles) is ringed by a conference of solemn pachyderms of plaster and sandstone, soapstone and granite.

When Meredith was nine years old, the same age as the children she now teaches, her mother Rhona took her to the hospital to visit her Auntie Pat, who had just given birth to the baby Rosemary (yes, that would be me). On the way to the hospital Meredith and her mother stopped at a newsagency to buy a card. Meredith, a tall child without ankles and with dimples for knees, was allowed to choose. She was drawn to a small square card with a marshmallow-pink pig surrounded by tufts of green grass, sporting a green polka-dot bow between its peaked ears. It was a happy-looking pig, and Meredith thought that the arrival of a cousin was a happy sort of occasion. She picked out the card and gave it happily to her mother, who crossly shoved it back down into the card rack, dog-earing a corner of it.

'You can't give a woman a card like that, Meredith! You might as well *call* her a pig!'

This was one of a number of psychic slaps that Rhona was unwittingly to give her daughter. Meredith has never forgotten that incident in the newsagency, and as a result of it is always careful not to buy greeting cards with images that might be considered, even in any obscure or tangential way, inappropriate. And every year on the last day of school, after defeating the pit-deep dread that makes her want to vomit or at least call in sick, she takes herself reluctantly to work. She smiles and thanks sincerely each exuberant gift-giver. But she thinks, as she unwraps each parcel, 'you might as well call me an elephant'.

> Elephants do not mate for life
> —*Elephant Information Repository*

For a time, Meredith had a boyfriend called Adrian Purdy. He was an information technology teacher at a high school adjacent to her primary school, and it is my strong suspicion that he never entirely discarded his teenage fascination with role-playing games. The internet filled the hole in his life which had opened when his old university mates moved on from Dungeons &

Dragons to golf. Although he and Meredith were together for many years, Adrian continued to live with his mother. This was largely because his mother took the view that couples who lived together before they were married did not deserve wedding presents. They had not, she said, sacrificed anything.

Jean Purdy had the long torso, short legs and lopsided gait that were, Adrian told Meredith, characteristic of female trolls. (Who were, Adrian told Meredith, the original 'trollops'.) Meredith found it hard not to picture Jean — especially when she delivered her doubt-free treatises on everything from the sanctity of smacking children to the benefits of fibre, the cure for leaf-curl in lemon trees and the cheek of indigenous people expecting apologies for things done in their best interests — standing beneath a bridge, her skull knobbled with horns.

Jean was as hard and defined as a stone, and she left Meredith feeling bruised. Jean was loud, while Meredith spoke as if she might diminish her size by keeping her voice small. Jean began dieting discussions with the prefix, 'Now I hope you won't mind me saying, but…' And behind those words Meredith heard the tearing of fabric, the ripping away of her veil of invisibility. Jean might as well have been saying: *Of course they notice, Meredith…rip…Do you really think anybody could be looking at you…rip…and not be thinking…fat… fat…FAT!*

After a while Meredith learned that when she heard 'Now I hope you won't mind me saying, but…' it was time to go. Her body remained there — monumentally there — in Jean's fussy Laura Ashley living room. But her mind departed the scene, leaving the soft flesh of the body to absorb the blows.

What Jean Purdy's son Adrian loved about Meredith was her flesh. He loved every gram and kilogram of it, would not have cared if she put on more weight, just as long as she didn't lose too much. It would be losing, he told her, too much of her self. She told me once, quietly, out the side of one of her chubby hands, that he could not stop himself, during lovemaking, from grasping at handfuls of her. Although she asked him, embarrassed, not to do it, he couldn't help himself.

Adrian Purdy's hands, like the rest of him, were unnaturally pale. They were unworked hands, with fingernails as soft as flakes of mica. With those hands he kneaded her like a cat kneading a pillow into shape. On the rare occasion he stayed the night at her house, his body forming a pale fringe around her, his hands still plied her flesh in his sleep.

Once, Meredith decided to tell Adrian the truth about the elephants. Although he had known her for several years, he had given her only a single elephant item: a jaffle-iron with a hard plastic lid in the shape of an elephant's face. And it was while Meredith was using the jaffle iron, after a morning in bed during which she had felt particularly close to him, that she realised it was the perfect moment to tell him. When he came out of the bathroom, she was going to say: *Adrian, I love this jaffle-maker, I really do. But the truth is, I really HATE elephants. Isn't that funny?* And she would laugh, and he would laugh, and they would laugh together in that kitchen-shaped bubble of intimacy. As it happened, Adrian Purdy emerged from the bathroom looking fixated and nervous. His pale hair was neatly combed at the sides but springing up at the crown. He put on his suede jacket and asked Meredith if they could skip breakfast, since there was something important they had to do.

Adrian drove, concentrating on the streets he travelled each day as if they had overnight become foreign. His soft nails flexed against the leather of the steering wheel. By the side of the river, he pulled over and turned to Meredith. Nervously, he fitted over her head the elastic of a sleeping mask. The sleeping mask was hers, she noted. She kept it in the bathroom for shutting out the light when she took long baths. She was momentarily put out that he had taken it without asking. When the car began to move again, Meredith could judge for a time, by the pattern of turns and roundabouts, where they were. Then she became uncertain, and lost her way.

After he parked, Adrian helped Meredith out of the car and took her by the hand. They walked a short way, and then she heard him whispering to someone and the sound of coins falling over each other into a pocket. He guided her through something that felt like a turnstile, cold metal touching her on her stomach and her flanks. She had to push herself through like a boiled egg through the neck of a bottle. Blindfolded, Meredith could smell food, and hear children. Adrian walked her along quickly, talking loudly about trust, and about the ability of the other senses to compensate rapidly for the loss of sight.

'Okay Mere, you can take it off now,' he said.

First there was the sunlight, which made her blink. Then, as her eyes slowly focused, the images that confronted her appeared, between blinks, as if in a slide show. She could almost hear the slides shunting through the carousel. And these are the things she saw:

1. Directly in front of her, Adrian Purdy, down on one knee, a shivering bunch of white daisies in one hand.

    click

2. A small child in a striped jumper, and in the child's hand, the stick of a toffee apple. The red bulb of the apple was swinging like a pendulum towards the earth, and the child's mouth, smeared red, was opened in glee.

    click

3. Behind Adrian Purdy, a cyclone fence.

    click

4. Over the cyclone fence, reaching, coming towards the shoulder of Adrian Purdy's suede jacket, a gently swaying prehensile trunk.

> An elephant family is led by a matriarch, with the matriarch being the oldest and most experienced of the herd
> *Elephant Information Repository*

My Auntie Rhona, my mother's oldest sister and Meredith's mother, does not remember the debacle with the pig card in the newsagency. If Meredith were to tell her about the lasting impact of the incident, Rhona would laugh good-naturedly and say, 'Oh, you silly girl! What funny things you remember!' She regards Meredith as her easiest child. She was always compliant, malleable, even-tempered and happy. She could almost have been pretty, with her flawless skin and shining curls a hair's breadth from black.

For Meredith's twenty-fifth birthday, Rhona planned a special gift. She had framed for Meredith an enlarged photograph of a female elephant on her knees by a waterhole, her trunk wrapped around the torso of a calf sinking into the mire. Rhona had been worried about her daughter. Although Meredith insisted she was fine, she had definitely been in low spirits since her abrupt and unexplained break-up with Adrian Purdy. Rhona was looking forward, in a quiet way, to the expression on Meredith's face when she unwrapped the photograph at her birthday party. The image spoke to Rhona of the extraordinary strength of her love for her daughter, of her determination to pull her through any kind of difficulty. And she was sure that Meredith, who was, bless her, so fond of elephants, would understand the message implicit in that coiled trunk.

> PINK ELEPHANT
> A hallucination, esp. as reputedly experienced by drunks
> —*Macquarie Dictionary*

I was there on the night of Meredith's birthday dinner (my gift to her was a pen in the shape of an elephant's head, the nib extruding from the tip of its trunk) and it seemed to me that all of Meredith's gathered friends were wearing lipstick a shade too bright, or a tie with a cartoon character grinning a little too insanely. They were determined not to allow the celebration to be affected by the absence of Adrian, and so they had brought with them to the little Thai restaurant their brightest, most shiny selves. Katrina King, as the closest friend, took the lion's share of the responsibility for being in high spirits and kept putting her arm around Meredith's shoulders and squeezing tight. Several of Meredith's friends were wondering why Meredith was not opening her birthday gifts. On a small table behind Meredith a pyramid was forming. At its base was a large flat parcel wrapped in handmade paper and affixed with a card that said *with love from Mum*. The fact was that Meredith was not opening her presents in case they robbed her of her resolve. She was going to do it. She had promised herself that she was going to stand up in front of her parents, her siblings, her closest friends and favourite colleagues, and confess to them that she did not particularly like elephants. And to this end, she had written for herself a speech:

Meredith's Speech

I have been searching for a collective noun for elephants. I know you're all thinking, *It's a* herd *of elephants, Meredith!* In my house, I have so many elephants that I need a collective noun larger than just four letters. I thought first of an 'engorgement' of elephants. Then I thought of a 'lumber' of elephants. Then I got it. What I have is a 'burden' of elephants.

You see, there has been a terrible mistake. I don't even really know myself how it started. Someone gave me an elephant, and then someone gave me another, and then everyone gave me elephants. I never chose elephants for myself, you see. I would not wish for you to think that I have not appreciated your gifts. Even if I am not especially fond of elephants, I am especially fond of all of you and I appreciate more than any material item in the world the love that came along with each and every one of those damned elephants. I have elephantiasis — the condition of being afflicted with too many elephants — and I ask you, as my family and my dearest friends, to help me find a cure.

Meredith's speech was short and, she hoped, sweet enough to save her — although she wondered if she should say the word 'damned' or leave it out for fear of offending Katrina King's fiancé, a religious minister in training.

It was a Tuesday night and the Thai restaurant was empty but for Meredith's party, which took up a long, thin table, broken into thirds by two enormous lazy Susans. Meredith and her friends and family had chosen the banquet menu. Staff cleared the remains of the savoury courses, taking away plates with leftover blobs of sweet chilli sauce and squeezed wedges of lime. Dessert — bananas poached in sweet coconut milk, lychees and a selection of ice-creams — was still to come, but for a moment the table was empty except for wineglasses and splotches of curry sauce on the pink tablecloth.

Meredith chose this clear, foodless moment between courses to stand up, clear her throat and unfold the single piece of paper she had held all night in her pocket, feeling its dangerous secret against her thigh almost as if it were a gun in its holster. Once she was on her feet, and the gathering had fallen silent, Meredith's bravado abandoned her. It left her standing, breathing heavily, thinking that perhaps she could just fold away the paper and say a few cobbled-together words of thanks and sit down again. Then she remembered Adrian Purdy at the zoo, kneeling between herself and an elephant named Bhutan, proposing marriage. Her resolve steeled again. She would have no more moments of her life destroyed by elephantiasis. So intent was she now upon her task that she ignored the noise going on in the restaurant foyer, and began.

'I have been searching for a collective noun for elephants. I know you're all thinking, *It's a* herd *of elephants, Meredith*!'

Sherrilyn Grey, a highly strung teacher's aide who spent Thursday afternoons in Meredith's room, emitted a snort of suppressed laughter. Meredith smiled appreciatively at Sherrilyn's acknowledgment of her wit.

'In my house, I have so many elephants that I need a collective noun larger than just four letters —'

The restaurant's sound system began to crackle with the first touch of a needle on vinyl and Meredith looked up to find that she had not had, and did not have, the attention of her guests. They were looking towards the foyer door as if they had become wax effigies of themselves.

The speakers nearly burst with the opening chords of a tune. *It isn't*, thought Meredith. And then she thought, *Oh God, it is*. And it was: *The Baby Elephant Walk*. Through the doorway came a saggy, baggy pink elephant. It was an elephant in two halves, like a circus horse, and the rear end was jack-knifing dangerously to the left. The guests on the opposite side of the table to where Meredith was standing parted in order to make room for the swaggering animal to approach.

The pink suit split in two. The halves rumpled to the floor

in two candy-pink shag-pile cocoons around the feet of blond men — their bronzed backs and buttocks bared — who swayed to comic lurches of the music. Hands clasped firmly over their crotches, they leaped onto the table and took their places on the twin lazy Susans. When they removed their hands, and spun around to face Meredith, she saw elephant ears fanning out over the elegram boys' washboard stomachs, the black circles inside plastic toy eyes spiralling inside their casing, turning around and around in time with the trunks, the long, grey, pink-tipped trunks rotating like tassels on a showgirl's nipples. Sherrilyn Grey was laughing so hard — mouth open, body shuddering — that her laugh had become soundless. Katrina King was dabbing at the corner of her eyes with a serviette which was almost the same shade as the electric blue mascara that was seeping down under her eyelids. Her fiancé doubled over in his seat and the skin on his face changed to the same colour as the hair of his silk-tie Yosemite Sam. The elegram boys swung their trunks to the left in unison, then the right in unison, then in opposite directions. They threw their trunks in the air and made trumpeting sounds. They smiled. Their perfect teeth glittered.

Auntie Rhona was feigning shock, hands over her eyes. The Thai waitresses in their narrow split-skirts of emerald green lined up along the bar, watching the spectacle, shrieking with mirth. The elegram boys performed the final flourish of their routine before leaping down from the table and positioning themselves to pose for photographs with the birthday girl. They flanked her tremendous bulk like a pair of pink and bronze bookends, their shimmering chests heaving lightly. For quite a long time nobody, not even those with their cameras trained on Meredith and the elegram boys, not even me (I am ashamed to say), but not Auntie Rhona either, noticed that Meredith — her face creased, her cheeks marked by slender tracks of tears — wasn't laughing.

TRAVEL

Rosie Little
in the Mother Country

This is a story that begins with the fact that my grandmother on the Little side was frightfully, frightfully English. Although she was prevailed upon, as a young bride, to immigrate to Australia, her Englishness proved quite impervious to the antipodean climate. When my father reached his late teens, Gran sent him 'back' to England to complete his education, being firmly of the opinion that while it was one thing to raise a son in a colony, it was quite another to allow yokels with rising inflections to reach him about Wordsworth. But despite Gran's best efforts, my father's Englishness was considerably more diluted than her own, and when the time came for him to send me off on my tour of duty to the Mother Country, it was for a holiday only. For the months between the end of school and the beginning of university, I was to stay with my godfather and his wife, a childless couple who lived in the countryside just out of London.

'The countryside just out of London,' I said to myself over and over in the excited weeks before I left. 'The countryside just out of London,' I told people behind the counters in shops, if they would listen. 'The countryside just out of London,' I told my friends, my vowels plumping up with each repetition.

The English countryside I knew well, for although I had never been out of Australia, my childhood had been filled with the kinds of books that had the word 'hedgerow' in the opening paragraph. I did not know specifically what a 'hedgerow' was, although I assumed it to be a cousin to the more prosaically named 'hedge'. But my ignorance was about to be rectified. I was about to see hedgerows, and primroses and brambles and cowslips (whatever the hell they were) and to discover, ambling about between them, darling little rabbits and hedgehogs that would eat nuts and berries from my hand.

On the day before I left, Gran gave me the address of her childhood home.

'It's not all that far from where you'll be staying. Go to see it if you get the chance. It'll stir something in you,' she said, pouring tea into her best china cups, the ones bearing the like-nesses of the Prince of Wales and Lady Diana Spencer.

Soon I was sitting at altitude, wearing synthetic airline socks and carefully peeling the foil lids from cups of orange juice and tiny packages of butter, determined not to overlook one single aspect of my adventure.

'The countryside just out of London,' I told the flight attendant, as well as the Asian gentleman sitting beside me, just in case he'd not heard me tell the flight attendant. When the cabin lights were dimmed, I pushed the button to recline my seat and began to review what I knew of the godfather into whose loving care I would be entrusted, in the countryside just out of London.

Details were sketchy. I knew that his name was Larry Trebilcock, and that he and my father had met within the hallowed halls of their respectably ancient university. I knew, too, that this sounded terribly *Brideshead Revisited*, but I assumed that my father and godfather had always been too interested in women to spend many summery riverside afternoons wearing cricket jumpers together. I knew that Trebilcock was pronounced 'tre-*bill*-coe', and that this was an English thing, like St John being pronounced 'sinjin' if it was a first or a middle name, but not if it came last. And that, I realised, was about all I actually knew.

I was met at Heathrow not by Larry, who was in an important business meeting in London, but by his wife Judy. She was a quiet and sandy-faced person who reminded me rather a lot of a flounder, and who had the childless woman's propensity to overfeed her cats. These gleaming and corpulent creatures were at the front door, mewing for second breakfast, when we pulled into the driveway of a vine-covered house, in the countryside…oh, you know.

Both the countryside and the house were as perfect as their counterparts in my seventeen-year-old imagination. On that day, the overcast sky seemed pressingly close, and the ground was covered with wet, satiny grass. I too felt all misty-moisty and soft-focused as I followed Judy through the small-windowed rooms of her home, around the winding paths of the garden and into the garage. In here was a skeletal Aston Martin, with various of its parts and panels piled up or leaning nearby. In a far corner, clear of where they might drip blood on any deep green duco, two headless pheasants were hanging by their feet from a clothesline.

'Lawrence shot those,' Judy said, her placid expression betraying neither pride nor disgust. 'He likes to go hunting on weekends.'

I should make it quite clear that I do not regard childlessness, *per se*, as a tragic state. In fact, I think that more people should probably give it a try. But tragic it was for Judy, who was unable to have children, yet would have been in her element with a tribe of quiet and sandy-faced kids to feed. She was the first woman I had ever met who was not a stay-at-home mum, but just a stay-at-home wife. I had no idea what this might entail, but I began to find out on that first evening, watching her as she moved around her kitchen like a slow dancer between stove-top and bench, her black cat and her ginger cat keeping perfectly in step as they purred around her slippered feet. She chopped and measured and mixed and simmered, and it was quite clear that neither our meal, nor the cats', was going to be an ordinary affair.

At the precise moment that Judy set down on the table the third of three beautifully garnished plates of sole in dill sauce, the front door opened. I smiled in readiness to greet my godfather, whom I'd last seen at my christening, back before I was able to focus my eyes particularly well. Now, however, I could see quite plainly that the man walking into the dining room was of average height, with straight fair hair, the majority of which was on the back of his head. In front, it receded from an owlish face set with thick glasses that shrank his eyes down to pin-pricks. Although he was wearing a suit, I could, if pushed, imagine him in knee-length breeches and a hound's-tooth hunting cap, a magnificently feathered bird slung over his shoulder.

'Hello Larry!' I said, leaping up from the table.

'Rosemary,' he said, nodding in my direction in a way that seemed not to invite hugging.

That was okay, we didn't have to hug. I sat down again.

'Rosie, please! Nobody calls me Rosemary. Not even Mum when she's cross. It's so lovely to be here, and to meet you again. I can't get over how perfect everything is. It's just how I imagined. I *love* your Aston Martin, by the way. Have you been working on it long?'

He raised his eyebrows and looked at his wife, who looked at me imploringly.

'Oh,' I said, putting a hand to my mouth as it dawned on me that she wanted me to hush.

Larry removed his blazer and placed it over the back of his chair, adjusting it so that its shoulders were equidistant from the edges of the chair-back. I observed a bit of tummy collapse over the waist of his pants and quiver like a poached egg does when it first hits the toast. He removed one cufflink, then the other, and dropped them one each into the left and right side pockets of his blazer. He rolled up his shirtsleeves — three quick tucks each side — then loosened his tie, and sat down at the table. I thought, for a moment, since Judy was sitting with her head slightly bowed and her hands in her lap, that we might be about to have grace. But then Larry picked up his knife and fork and began to flake apart the fish on his plate.

And so we ate, and did not speak. Our speechlessness amplified all the small noises of a meal: the squeaks of silver on china, the setting down of a wineglass on a coaster, the muted chewing of soft fish-flesh. I became aware of a rhythm to Larry's mastication and started to keep count. He chewed twenty times per mouthful, rarely more or less, although sometimes he paused to purse his lips and extrude a small white fish-bone and place it, at a regular interval from the last, on the scalloped rim of his china plate. Soon all that remained of his meal was the frame of the fish and this tidy parade of curving bones. As his knife and fork clattered together on the plate, I breathed out in relief, certain that now conversation would begin in earnest.

'What's for dessert?' he asked.

'I hadn't planned —' Judy began.

'Sorry?'

'Your cholesterol? Remember, Dr Maxwell said…and we talked about your cutting back?'

'Plums and ice-cream, please.'

'I'm sorry, love, but we haven't any plums.'

'No plums?'

'No, no plums.'

He sat for a moment, thinking, and pursing his lips in the same way as he had done to eject his fish bones.

'Why, Judith, have we no plums?'

'We finished all the ones I preserved.'

'You didn't think, perhaps, to get some more?'

'The last time I was at Tescos they hadn't any plums either.'

'I am given to understand that you went to a major supermarket and were unable to obtain plums?'

'I'm very sorry, love, but if they don't have plums, well, they don't have plums. There's not much I can do about it.'

'Then I suppose I shall have to have prunes.'

'Rosie?'

I could already imagine the prune stones nestling in the scalloped edging of the dessert bowl.

'Nothing for me. Thanks.'

Breakfast, I thought, would be the ideal opportunity for a second attempt at becoming warmly reacquainted with my godfather. Perhaps, on the previous evening, he'd been tired after a long day at work. Perhaps his meeting had gone very badly. Perhaps certain stone fruits were his only hope for expelling the substantial carrot that appeared to have been shoved up his arse.

'Good morning, Larry,' I said brightly when he arrived at the table and selected a piece of toast from the rack placed there only seconds earlier by Judy.

'Rosemary.'

'What excitement does your day hold?'

'Ex*cite*ment? I'm going to work.'

'Well, if not exciting, will it be a productive day, perhaps?'

'Here,' he said, handing me a section of the newspaper Judy had set down beside his breakfast plate. 'This should be to your taste.'

He had folded it open to the comics. I pointedly turned over to the opinion page and, for quite some time, tried to engage with the various debates that were being furthered in the paper's small dense type.

'What does supercilious mean?' I asked absent-mindedly, my mouth full of toast and jam.

'Why?' he asked, through the grey tissue of the financial pages. 'Who called you that?'

True, it was not quite the reception I'd expected. But I didn't let it get me down; Judy was friendly enough, and I was sure Larry would come around eventually. In the meantime, London was just a short, speeding train ride away.

In the Underground I was Alice, tumbling through the blackened rabbit-holes of the city. I was a child in Willy Wonka's chocolate factory, hurtling along bright-coloured tubes as they bent and weaved through space at map-neat angles. Wherever in the city I was, I was never far from a magic portal that could take me somewhere else. In Covent Garden, I watched a man dislocate both shoulders in order to pass his body through a stringless tennis racket. In Oxford Street, I bought a brand new pair of sixteen-hole, cherry-red Doc Martens and a hot chocolate. I leafed through, but could not afford, the wares of the antiquarian bookshops of Charing Cross Road. In Trafalgar Square I got pigeon shit in my hair.

But if, in the Mother Country, I had found myself in a kind of Wonderland, then chief among the strange creatures whose unpredictable manners I did not understand was my godfather himself.

'Where are you going today?' Larry asked me one morning, as I stood in his hallway putting on my coat.

'I thought I might go and look at the house where Gran grew up. It's not too far from here, apparently,' I said.

'Is it necessary, do you think,' he began, leaning in so close behind me that I could smell his breath, 'for the purpose of visiting your grandmother's childhood home, to dress like a kindergarten whore?'

'Sorry?'

My outfit, comprised of findings from a week's worth of rabbit-hole journeys through London, involved the cherry-red Doc Martens, a pair of torn denim hotpants from the Camden Markets, some Union Jack tights from Soho and a frothy shirt with lace ruffles at the sleeves that I had unearthed at Portobello Road. Only my red duffle coat had come from home. Now I buttoned it up, right to the neck, blushing brightly enough to match it.

'Don't be any later than five o'clock,' Larry said, tweaking a hank of my hair before he walked out the door.

Of course my mother had told me — as all mothers tell their girls at some stage — that the only reason boys pull girls' hair is because they like them but don't know how to say so. But I needed clarification. Was this, I wondered as I walked to the train station, a truism that applied equally well to middle-aged men as to schoolboys?

By this stage in my travels, I had learned a little about British public transport etiquette. I was getting pretty good at avoiding eye contact, ignoring beggars and sidestepping spruikers. But on the day I set off for my grandmother's house, there was sitting opposite me an old woman who did not seem to know that it was rude, on trains, to look people right in the face.

She was a very small person and she wore a dress that was black with white polka-dots, but which had at the throat a large, floppy bow that was white with black dots. She sat not in the way that most of the other travellers did — right back in their comfortless seats, slouched and with their heads in their books/earphones/personal reveries — but on the very edge of her seat, her buckled hands resting together on the handle of an umbrella. Its canopy was also black with white polka-dots, although these dots, I noticed, were of a marginally greater circumference than those on her dress. Her hair was bright white and her shoes were tiny black lace-ups with a not-inconsiderable heel. She was so marvellous that I wanted to stare at her, but I couldn't, since she was already staring at me. So I took in her image in flickers, my eyes gathering just a little more information each time my gaze moved from the port to the starboard windows and back again. I loved how her saggy cheeks were punctuated with glaring circles of reddish rouge, and how badly painted were her lips. I tried to read her life story from her wrinkles, but could not decide whether her face was set in an expression of concern, or amusement, or an equal mixture of the two.

A Word from Rosie Little
ON FACIAL LINES

No doubt your mother, or some other responsible adult in your life, warned you about pulling faces when a change in wind direction was on the cards. Of course, the idea that you could end up with the tip of your tongue lodged permanently in a nostril just because the breeze swung to the east sounds as ridiculous as green vegetables putting hairs on your chest, or the marrow in your bones melting because you sat with your back too close to the fire. But on reflection (my own reflection, as it happens, in my very own bathroom mirror), I've decided that the saying about pulling faces is not an *entirely* silly one after all.

Get on a bus full of old people and you'll understand what I mean. It's easy to pick the woman who's spent her life indulging herself in moral indignation, tightening her lips against mothers who are too young, mothers who are too old, young men with dangerous-looking haircuts, and Winifred Martin going off with May Charleston's husband, and at their age, honestly. Yes, you'll be able to pick her in a trice, since she'll be the one with the cat's arse where her mouth ought to be.

I once met a monk called Father Basil and I can attest to the fact that a life of contemplation does magnificent things for your skin in old age. Sit around all day with a beatific smile on your face, pondering the beauty of nature and the essential goodness of humanity, and you really will end up with your face permanently set in an expression of deep serenity. It's too late for me, of course, to achieve such a thing. At just past thirty, I've already laid the groundwork for my old woman's face, and what with all the bemused and quizzical faces I've affected in my time, I'm bound to be a very puzzled-looking octogenarian. Oh, that wind is out there all right. It just takes a few years for it to change you.

*

'Enjoying your travels?' the polka-dot woman asked directly.

'Who me?' I feigned, but the glitter in her eye told me that she was not taken in. 'Am I really that obviously a tourist?'

'Do you see anyone else looking out the windows?'

'Oh.'

'But you appear to be having a good adventure. And adventure is good for the soul, don't you find?'

'Absolutely!' I said, coming swiftly to the opinion that this woman was every bit as wonderful as her eccentric outfit. I was willing to bet she would know the answer to the hair-tweaking question.

'This next town is very picturesque. I'm sure you'd love it.'

'I'm sure I would too, but my stop is four on from here.'

'I like your boots,' she said, her smile a dare.

'I like your whole ensemble,' I rejoined, and she closed her eyes as she effected a slow curtsey with her head.

As the train slowed into the next station, I caught sight of the latticed windows of its village shops and a man with a pipe walking a cobbled street with a sheepish border collie at his side. Enchanted, I jumped up from my seat just in time to clip the train's exit button and have the sliding doors open out onto a scene straight off an English biscuit tin. And as I stepped off the train, the polka-dot woman caught my eye, and winked.

In the village, I took tea and sent postcards and bought the kinds of sweets desired by girls on their way to a new term at boarding school. I wandered across an ancient bridge and down a grassy way to a riverbank, resting upon which was a very large white swan. There had been a swan in the slender illustrated storybook Gran had given to me one Christmas of my childhood: the story of a girl whose father went to sea and left her in the care of a terrible old woman who didn't feed her enough, and who allowed her clothes to turn into rags that the girl herself was forced to mend, at night, by candlelight. The swan came to the girl's rescue, however, bringing her bread scraps in the basket he carried in his beak and, finally, allowing her to ride on his broad feathered back as he flew out over the sea to greet her father's returning ship. I approached the living replica of my fictional swan, already imagining how soft its feathers would feel as I stroked the noble curve of its head. But when the swan saw me coming, it reared up to form a cave of white feathers that seemed higher than I was tall. I had never thought of a swan as behaving otherwise than tranquilly, but here was one flapping wildly and almost growling, whipping an angry beak about on the end of a long mobile neck. I turned and ran, but the swan chased me and lashed out to strike me on the bum.

'Gosh, I saw that. Are you all right?' called a tallish boy coming down the bank towards me from the place where a book was splayed out, face down on a park bench.

'That must have looked quite funny,' I said, embarrassed that my stupidity had had an audience.

'Funny? No, swans can be vicious. Snap a kiddie's arm with that beak.'

'It's going to be a good bruise,' I said, rubbing the buttock that would indeed, over the next few days, bloom impressively in shades of purple and green.

'You're not from here,' the boy said, looking quite pleased.

'Clearly not.'

'What are you, Aussie or Kiwi?' he asked, beginning a conversation that swiftly lapped the globe, took in the title of the book he'd been reading, traversed the oeuvres of our favourite writers and circled back to land on the subject of our names.

'Julian,' he said, and the hand he offered felt warm and clean.

My nose was level with his sternum and, since his ribbed jumper smelled of the kind of washing powder only a mother would use, I felt quite safe.

'Rosie,' I said.

On the riverbank, we continued to talk. And then we adjourned to the darkened interior of a small pub that I did not confess to being eleven and a half months too young to enter. Nothing on tap behind the sturdy oaken bar was familiar, and none of the names on the cans in the fridge meant anything to me either (except XXXX, which I knew that no real Australians drank anyway).

'I've got no idea,' I said. 'What would you be having if you weren't driving?'

'Snakebite and black,' he said.

'Which is?'

'Cider, lager and blackcurrant juice.'

Remembering Rene Pogel, I did a quick cocktail safety check, but could discern no particular threat in Kcalb dna Etibekans.

'One of those then,' I said. 'Thank you.'

I sipped so slowly that my pint of snakebite and black lasted for all the time that it took for us to tell each other our whole lives. And just before I was going to be late getting back, Julian drove me home in his tinny little car. Outside Larry and Judy's house, he settled a hand protectively on top of mine.

'I have two little sisters, you know, and I would hate to think that either of them would ever get into a car with a strange man like you've just done. I want you to promise me that you won't ever do it again.'

It was funny to hear this sweet boy refer to himself as a strange man, but his face was so serious that I resisted the temptation to giggle. Instead, I risked a quick kiss on his cheek, and dashed up the path to the front door, wondering how, exactly, I was going to describe to Larry and Judy my gran's childhood home.

Over the next few weeks, I determined that my mother's hair-pulling advice did not apply in this case. Larry most definitely did not like me. On some days he treated me in the same indifferent manner he treated Judy, and on other days he flustered himself up into a performance of patriarchal zeal, all curfews and rules and telling me to tidy my room.

I did feel sorry for him that he had no children of his own to discipline (well, okay, not *that* sorry), but at seventeen I felt too old to be told which train to catch and what time to be home. And was it my imagination, or was his behaviour becoming increasingly erratic at roughly the same rate that I was getting to know Julian?

I always think of getting to know Julian as like being let loose in a confectioner's workshop. He had the kind of caramel skin that it is unfair for English people of Caucasian origin to own, given the climate they live in, and his honey-coloured hair flopped down over his eyebrows into rum and raisin eyes.

I spent hours nibbling at his lips, which were large and impossibly plush, pale-pink and soft, like pillows of Turkish delight. Remembering my classmate Geoffrey Smethurst's dichotomy of penis dimensions, I assumed that Julian's was on the long and thin side of things. But it wasn't revolting. At all. When you first touched it, it was mushroom-coloured and pliable as marzipan. And then, quite rapidly, not like that at all. One afternoon in Julian's bedroom, when I had been playing with this marvellously changeable sweetmeat for quite some time, it alarmed me by making a warm puddle in the palm of my hand. The contents of the puddle were kind of gelatinous, and kind of creamy, but not even a bit like toothpaste. I wondered if there were any other major surprises still to come.

There were.

In a bordello-like cinema that had beanbags and couches in the place of seating banks, with my legs and tongue twisted around Julian's matching parts, I began to shiver. But not the kind of shiver that puckers your skin into gooseflesh. In fact, not the kind of shiver I'd ever shivered before. It moved through my body, seeming to inject my bloodstream with some kind of magical cordial as it went. I was flooded with warmth, first in my pelvis, then in my stomach, and then somewhere dangerously close to my heart. I was sure that if I looked down at my wrists in the darkness, I would be able to see my veins picked out in pulsing blue light. What the hell was *that*? I wondered.

I thought that I could successfully conceal these newfound pleasures beneath winter clothes and a girlish manner. But now I suspect that those little blue lights, which began to pulse whenever I so much as thought of Julian, were visible to others in the small margin of flesh between my cuffs and the heels of my hands, and that they probably showed at the throat, too.

One morning during those days of getting to know Julian, I stood in the shower deciding that I had always accepted too readily the wisdom of Geoffrey Smethurst.

'I mean, you're *cute*, but you'll never be exactly *sexy*,' he'd told me once on the bus on the way home, as he compared me with our exquisite, buxom, part-Brazilian drama teacher.

Julian thought I was sexy. He'd told me so. Although I doubted that I would share this with Geoffrey. If we ended up at university together, I would just give him the odd superior smile.

The shower was of the pathetic, drizzly English kind, in which you don't exactly have to run around in order to get wet, but you do have to alternate your body parts under the water in order to stay mostly warm. I was doing this, and practising my superior smile, when I heard the *bathroom* door open. I knew that Judy would already be at the markets, buying the day's provisions. Larry, I thought, would have left to go shooting with his brother. But here was the shape of him, including the peak of his hunting cap, visible through the thin membrane of the shower curtain. I stood very still, feeling triply naked, and soon I was cold everywhere.

'Where are you going today?' he asked.

'Actually, I wasn't planning to go anywhere,' I said, the arms I wrapped around my chest making me feel no less exposed.

'You're not going out?'

I measured in my mind the metres between the end of the shower curtain and a big green towel hanging on its rack on the wall.

'No, no, just staying around here,' I said, trying to sound normal, and wondering why this seemed as if it were an important thing to do.

For what seemed like a long time he stood there, although I couldn't hear anything except water trickling around my ears, not even the sound of him breathing.

Christmas wasn't so much white as crystalline. Stretched across the narrow window of my bedroom at Larry and Judy's house was a spider's web threaded with sparkling beads of ice, and through it I could see the lawn frozen into spikes. Downstairs, there was a single, lonely present under the potted Christmas tree on the sideboard. It was for me.

'Merry Christmas,' said Judy, as I unwrapped the gift of a pair of lamb's wool slippers. Guiltily. I was almost certain that she didn't know about the gift I'd already received, the one I'd found at the end of my bed when I'd woken: a three pack of Marks & Spencer underpants (white, embroidered, dainty) that wasn't wrapped, but had a gift tag that read 'FROM SANTA' in Larry's uptight capital letters. He had been in my room when I was asleep. Ick. I bundled the knickers into a discreet compartment of my suitcase in the hope that out of sight would soon transpose into out of mind.

Lunch, held in the formal dining room and attended by Judy's parents and Larry's aged mother, involved a Royal

Worcester dinner service, two pheasants with chestnut stuffing, and an entire vegetable patch roasted to perfection.

'You are so lucky, Lawrence,' said his mother from beneath her orange crepe-paper hat. 'Judy is the most superb cook.'

'Why do you think I married her?' he asked, carving into the voluminous breast of a bird.

Nobody laughed or smiled. Maybe it wasn't even meant to be a joke.

It was on Christmas night, at Julian's place, while his parents were safely turkey-and-red-wine replete in their part of the house and his younger sisters asleep, that I got the present I really wanted.

'Have you done this before?' Julian asked me after a couple of moist hours of petting, his naked and caramel-skinned body poised for entry.

'Technically, yes. Effectively, no. What about you?'

'Not even technically, I'm afraid,' he said, trying to coordinate himself to hang onto the base of the condom and find the right spot at the same time.

'Oh no,' I said, catching sight of the time on his wristwatch. 'It's already midnight.'

'Mmmm?'

'I'm supposed to be back by now.'

'Oh, you want to go?' he asked, disappointed but polite as ever, as he pulled away.

'No, no,' I said, taking matters into my own hands.

'You should go.'

'Shhh,' I said, kissing his Turkish delight lips.

'What will you tell Larry?'

'I will tell him the truth.'

'You will not.'

'I will. I will tell him the honest-to-goodness, absolute truth.'

'What?'

'I will tell him,' I said, 'that I was out in the woods, picking flowers.'

Three hours beyond my curfew, light in the head and sticky between the legs, I stood on the footpath outside Larry and Judy's. Avoiding the dead giveaway of the white gravel path, I crossed over the grass and went quietly through the garage — past the place where the Christmas pheasants had bled onto the floor — and around to the French doors that led into the living room. Slowly, slowly, slowly, I pushed down on the handle and eased the door open into the muffling thickness of the drawn curtains within. Quietly, I slipped through the gap in the curtains to find Larry, sitting in his pyjamas, dressing-gown and slippers, waiting up for me. The lights in the room were dimmed. Someone like Carly Simon sang a smoky song through the speakers of the stereo.

'I can just imagine what you've been up to,' Larry said.

As he came towards me, I backed away, and soon he was between me and the door I'd just come through. His owlish face, normally quite waxy and pallid, was flushed as if he'd drunk too much port.

'While you are here in my house, I am responsible for you, and I cannot have you out behaving like a wanton little slut,' he said, with a disturbing amount of relish.

'I am not having this conversation with you,' I replied, trying to keep my voice steady even though I was shaking and could feel my pulse everywhere, even in the tips of my ears.

'I am in *loco parentis* here, and I have no intention of sending you home to your father pregnant,' he hissed.

'Well you are completely *loco* if you think that I'm going to let you talk to me like this. My *father* doesn't talk to me like this.'

'What you need, you smart-mouthed little tart, is a good ——' He lunged at me. '—— spanking.'

But I was too quick for him. I was up the stairs and behind the locked door of my room before he could catch me.

I was safe. But trapped, since even if I'd been prepared to find a way down from the upper-storey window, its double-glazed security panels opened out only a few inches. I could hear, out in the hallway, the sound of Larry placing a call on his rotary dial telephone. He was dialling an awful lot of numbers, and I realised that because of the time difference, it was not an even slightly unreasonable hour at which to ring my parents. He would catch them on the back deck, eating sandwiches full of leftover ham, while they listened on the radio to the Boxing Day test.

'Nymphomania,' I heard Larry tell my mother (another word I would not have been familiar with if it had not been for Geoffrey Smethurst), and 'inappropriate behaviour', along with 'might need to get some professional help'. None of which bothered me half as much as when I heard him say 'and the odd bit of cash has gone missing out of Judith's purse, too'.

*

And so it was that my adventure in the Mother Country was cut short. Although special dispensation was granted for me to have a stilted and supervised lunch with Julian before I was plunged, lily-white and lovesick, into the sudden, roasting, red-brick heat of a suburban Australian January. Mum and Dad took me to a counsellor who pronounced me quite normal, but it took a while, nonetheless, for the trace of suspicion to disappear from my parents' faces when they looked at me with loving concern.

'What exactly *happened*?' my mother asked repeatedly during the weeks I spent indoors with the curtains drawn, oscillating between wilting and pining.

Everything, I wanted to say. But then, not really anything at all. There were no fingerprints. There was no evidence. Even the underpants looked innocent with their forget-me-not trim.

'He does care about you, darling, he's your godfather,' she said.

'Not anymore he's not,' was all I would say.

What had my parents seen in him, I wondered? What had been the basis of their friendship? I took down the baby-pink album from a high shelf in my parents' den and found the images I was looking for on the third or fourth page of my life. There was a picture of me, my face a small, indistinct disc somewhere near the top of a smocked layette. There was a picture of my christening cake, shaped and intricately iced in the image of a baby's pram. There were pictures of my parents, sometimes separately, but mostly standing together in matching purple outfits. And there was Larry, holding me out at arm's length as he made his solemn C of E vow to keep me on the straight and narrow. I wanted to snatch my infant self away from him. How would I ever forgive my parents for not only inviting the bad fairy to my christening, but delivering me straight into his hands?

In fact it was only very recently that I did forgive them. Properly. And for that, we must thank my mother's conversion to the scrapbooking craze. Pinking shears and cropping tools blazing, she took to my baby pictures, and then gave me the revamped collection for my birthday. Perhaps it was the new layout that made me see the photos of my christening differently. Or maybe it was simply the passing of time. Either way, by now the photos stirred up nothing more than curiosity. Which of the crimes my parents had committed on the day of my christening, I wondered, should be considered the more unforgivable? Appointing Larry Trebilcock as my godfather, or dressing the way they did for the occasion? It was even possible, I realised, that each of these lapses of judgment could be made explicable in the light of the other. For if you could choose to attend your baby daughter's christening in a flared purple suit and a psychedelic black and magenta tie — with your facial hair trimmed, I might add, into the beard-but-no-moustache combination known as the Amish or Abe Lincoln style — then surely you could make dubious choices about friendships. And if you could imagine that you looked fetching in a purple crepe dress with a white ruffle around the edge of the bodice, it might also be possible for you to imagine that

Larry Trebilcock was a good sort of a chap to be made responsible for a girl-child's spiritual guidance. Amish beards once were the height of fashion. *Ergo*, Larry might once have seemed a good candidate to be godfather to one's only daughter. Fashions change, after all.

BEAUTY

The Wardrobe

On the day Justine moved in with Henri, he pushed the clothes in his wardrobe to one side to make room for hers. The wardrobe, with its oak-heavy doors closed, had looked to be an antique. But inside was a modern maze of shelving and compartments, all of which were filled with clothes that seemed to Justine to be weighty with quality. There were jumpers — black, cream, caramel and toffee — in softest alpaca, or else in thick-spun merino, densely cabled. There were jackets in supple suede and leather, and a woollen winter coat lined with black fur as luxuriant as a bear's. The coat-hangers of dark polished timber looked expensive as well.

Justine had left behind everything but her nicest and most favourite things, but even these seemed tatty hanging in the wardrobe next to Henri's clothes. Thinning patches showed in cheap cotton, as did the pilling on part-synthetic jumpers. She could see the unevenness of her hems and how her seams frayed for lack of finishing.

'You don't really wear this,' Henri said without a question mark, singling out a beige cardigan.

'I don't?'

'Jus*tine*.'

It was ribbed, tweedy, and made mostly out of real wool. It had been loose to start with, but was now stretched at the side seams from being hung on the line. It had a wide collar and knobbly buttons that Justine now saw, for the first time, were woven out of vinyl and not leather. Not that she would have cared even if she had noticed before. It was a cardigan for being relaxed and comfortable and having nothing important to do. It was a Sunday cardigan.

'You'd look like something out of *Starsky & Hutch*,' he said, tugging the cardigan off its hanger. It more than filled the small bin in the corner of his bedroom, one of its sleeves reaching over the side as if waving for rescue. But Justine was not paying attention. Soon all of the clothes she was wearing, and all of the clothes he was wearing, were heaped on the floor beside his bed, and she was thinking how, even when he was undressed, he was better covered than her. Hung next to his in a wardrobe, she thought, her pale and freckled skin would look as threadbare as her clothes.

In the first few days that she lived with Henri, Justine spent time delving her toes into the deep green plush of his carpet, padding over tiles of his bathroom floor, and wondering if any of these surfaces would ever feel as if they belonged to her. The decision to leave home had been an easy one. The only difficult thing had been the discussion with her mother, who had just looked down into the squares of her newspaper crossword puzzle when Justine asked her what she thought.

'Well?' Justine had prodded.

'I'm not sure. That's all.'

'You think I'm too young.'

'It's not that.'

'I'm nineteen years old. You were *married* by now.'

'It's not that,' her mother had said, looking up at last. 'Perhaps it's just that I'll miss you.'

'You always knew I would go. Nobody stays out here. Well, nobody except Jill.'

Her mother had not leapt to the defence of her elder daughter (who showed no signs of moving on from her job in the local video store). She had simply sighed, indicating that she was, as ever, their incontrovertibly and irritatingly impartial referee.

'I thought that when you went it would be for university, or for a job. Not for a man.'

'He's more interesting than guys my age. He knows all about things.'

'I love you, darling, and I worry for you. That's all.'

'You don't like him.'

'We barely know him,' her mother had said, and Justine had known herself to be included in the 'we'.

Henri worked long hours, and in the evenings before he arrived home Justine walked the stairs between the storeys of the tall and narrow house, counting each of the steps in an effort to own them. She noticed how the green plush was flattened in the centre of each step between the lowest storey and the middle storey of the house, but on the stairs that led up to the attic it was as good as new. The attic was neither secret nor locked, only cold and disused, nothing in it but some old department store mannequins. They had been stranded there by a deal gone wrong. Henri often bought things cheaply and sold them at a profit: the walls of a long passageway in the house were presently taken up with bolts of luscious imported fabrics. The buyer of the mannequins, Henri explained, had gone broke before the deal went through.

The mannequins disturbed Justine. She didn't like the way they bore their dismemberment so casually. The ebony girl balanced her torso on the locking pin that would have joined her to the racehorse legs that stood beside her.

A woman's upper body, its bald head the colour of stocking gussets, lay face down and parallel to its disconnected legs. Justine felt for the redhead most of all, because she reminded her of herself. She swivelled the mannequin's wig around the right way so that the edge of her thick, matted fringe rested on her painted eyebrows, and tried to find her missing arm. There was a pile of limbs in the corner, the paint of their skin chipping away from fingers and toes, but Justine couldn't find one to match the redhead's fair, pinkish skin.

Not long after the cardigan incident, Henri took Justine to a smart street in the city, to a boutique with shop girls as thin as straps of liquorice. One had a long ponytail and wore a miniature black dress and retro high heels. The other wore flares ruffled from the knees down and her hair in a sharp quiff that put Justine in mind of a shark fin. These women would be the type, Justine thought, to factor in the calories in the sugar-coating of their contraceptive pills. They greeted Henri like a pair of cats on heat, kissing his cheeks in the European style and brushing his lapels with their slender hands. Justine hung back in the doorway, taking in the opulence of the dressing-room drapes and the size of the gilt-framed mirrors, and wondering just how many other women Henri had brought here to shop.

'A redhead?' asked the ponytail girl, as if it were an unlikely choice.

'I like them fiery,' said Henri, grasping Justine by the waist, and the ponytail raised a dextrous and sceptical eyebrow.

'So we'll be staying away from most of the oranges, the pinks and the reds,' said the shark fin, making clacking noises with coat-hangers as she began flicking through the racks.

'And leaning towards rich creams, chocolate browns and greens, lovely greens,' said the ponytail, her voice melodious over the percussive clicks.

'Oh this, yes, this,' said the shark fin, pulling out a swish of soft green with striped ribbon trimming at the capped sleeves and at the waist.

'The martini dress. Oh, yes! You must have that. And this,' said the ponytail, bringing out a fitted coat in cream linen densely embroidered with burnished flowers and green leaves. 'Which would go with *these*,' said the shark fin, placing by Justine's feet a pair of knee-high and high-heeled brown backless boots with square toes and brogue patterning.

'Perfect,' sighed the ponytail.

The shark fin held out a long, floating shirt in teal-coloured silk and Justine liked the forgiving width of its soft, draping folds.

'That's nice,' she ventured, but Henri shook his head.

He nodded to a snug black brocade pants suit and an olive knit bolero and a wispy evening gown with a split framed by feathers; to a passing parade of tight pants and skirts, tops, jumpers, dresses, wraps, shoes and stockings. Justine came from a family of statuesque women who referred to themselves as 'big-boned'. But to wear the sleek and fitted pieces Henri was selecting, she would need to be an X-ray.

'You don't think I should try these things on?' she said, when the counter was piled with linen and satin and velvet and lace, and when the floor was stacked with boxes of shoes.

'They'll fit,' he said.

'I'm not always the same size in tops and bottoms.'

'Don't worry. They'll fit.'

'There's no way I'll get into this,' she said, holding up the martini dress and looking in all the usual places for a size label, finding it in none. 'This couldn't be more than a ten, and I haven't worn size ten anything since I was at high school.'

'Ah, you'd be surprised.'

'Trust him, hon,' said the shark fin at the cash register. 'Henri's a real wizard with fit.'

Henri put all of her new clothes away in the wardrobe himself, folding jumpers into shop-perfect squares and evenly spacing the hanging garments, similar colours together, fronts all facing the same way. And then, when he had finished, he lay back against the pile of bolsters and pillows at the head of his bed and asked: 'May I have the pleasure?'

'We haven't even talked about how much all this cost.'

This had been worrying her all day, sitting in the bottom of her stomach like the feeling she got when (contrary to her father's firm principle) she signed something without reading the fine print first.

'Why would you want to have a dull conversation like that when you've got a wardrobe full of new clothes to try on?' he said, smiling indulgently.

'So I don't need to worry?'

'No, you don't need to worry.'

But although the feeling was leavened, it did not disappear entirely.

'Okay then. Well, what do you want to see first?' she asked, manufacturing an extra degree of enthusiasm that had failed to arise naturally.

'Whatever pleases m'lady.'

She chose the martini dress, slipping it off its polished timber hanger and stretching out the waistline between her hands. It was tiny. There was no way. She pulled at the fabric again, but there was no give in it. Oh well, she thought, he would soon see what happened when you bought a woman clothes without having her try them on first. With the amount he must have spent, they would surely exchange. But when she slipped the green dress over her head, the fabric fell easily down over her rib-cage, tucked in to her waist, and flowed over her hips as if it had been made to fit no other body than her own. She twirled in the mirror, piled her hair on her head with her hands and twirled again.

'It's beautiful,' she said, although what she was thinking was *I'm beautiful*, and the mirror reflected her delight and surprise.

Justine's friends came down on cheap flights for a long weekend and she met up with them for lunch in the city.

'Oh my God, Justine, you look fantastic!'

'You've lost so much weight. In a good way. You look amazing.'

'I hardly recognised you. You look so chic.'

'What have you done to your hair?'

'Where did you get that dress? It must have cost a mint!'

'Look at your *nails*. Are they fake?'

'You've definitely been going to the gym.'

'They're not what I think they are. Are they? Are you kidding? They're *real*? They are real Manolo Blahniks and Henri bought them for you himself? You didn't even pick them out?'

'What, he pays for everything? And you don't even have to pay him back? There's got to be a catch. Is he kinky in bed or something?'

'Speaking of kinky, do you know what Manolo Blahnik calls that little line where your toes press up against each other? He calls it "toe cleavage".'

'He's a shoemaker. It's his business to be a foot fetishist.'

'Are they comfortable? I don't think I could walk in them. I'd never be able to go anywhere, I'd just have to sit around looking decorative.'

'He bought you two pairs? What are the other ones like? Go on, describe. Every detail. Please tell me they come in red too.'

'Talk about falling on your feet.'

'Where do you *find* a man like that? I'm moving to this city. That's it. Definitely.'

'A man who buys you clothes. And shoes. And clothes and shoes like that. You hang on to that man, Juz.'

A Word from Rosie Little
ON THE SHOE GODDESS

Either you are, or you are not, one of the Shoe Goddess's chosen ones. And, as it happens, I am. What does this mean? Well, let's say that I have visited a shop and seen a pair of shoes that I like, but left without buying them. If the Shoe Goddess wants me to have these particular shoes, then she will whisper to me, for several days 'the *red* shoes, the *red* shoes, the *red* shoes' (if, in fact, the pair in question is red — which often, in my case, it is). She will whisper for about a week, by which time I have usually got the message and returned to the shop to pick up the shoes, knowing that they are cosmically destined to be mine.

I have learned, though, through bitter experience, that if I fail to follow the divine guidance of the Shoe Goddess, I will be punished. The very next time I spy a pair of adorable shoes, the Shoe Goddess will intervene to ensure that they are available in every size but mine. Or, she will simply abandon me to my own judgment and allow me to buy a pair of bad shoes that are some combination of uncomfortable, unflattering and far too expensive. If, on the other hand, I listen to her words of wisdom, I will be rewarded. Perfect shoes will be on sale, or the last pair in the shop will be in my size. I must have pleased her tremendously once, for she directed me to a shop that sold very cheap sample shoes, each and every one of which was size six and a half. Can you imagine, an entire shop full of shoes in nothing but your own size? Bliss!

But, you know, there are always those who take things too far. When all's said and done, shoe fetishism is an *ism*, and we all know how people can lose their heads over those. You might think that Imelda Marcos was a true devotee of the Shoe Goddess, simply by virtue of the vast number (some say

3000, but she has only admitted to 1060) of pairs of size eight and a half shoes found in her Manila mansion after the coup of 1986. But I doubt that the Shoe Goddess approved of her at all. Personally, I don't believe that the Shoe Goddess wants anyone to own more pairs of shoes than they can wholeheartedly love at one time. And she certainly wouldn't want shoes to be confined for months and months on end to even the nicest or most cleverly designed of shoe racks. She would be conflicted about shoes being held captive in museums, too, for while she would argue that people should have the opportunity to admire the great shoes of history in three dimensions, she would, in her heart of hearts, rather that they were out being worn down to nothing on the feet of women who loved them.

*

Justine had been living with Henri for three months when he announced that he had to go overseas on business. She half-expected that he would leave her with a ring of heavy keys and a prohibition against entering the smallest room in the house. But he only gave her a copy of his itinerary and told her not to forget to arm the security system when she went out.

One weekend while he was away she took his car, a sleek black creature with wide leather seats and arm rests, and drove all the way home. She couldn't listen for long to the cymbal-clashing discordance of the orchestral music he had in the CD player, so she switched over to the radio, losing and finding stations as she left the city behind and crossed the state border, heading inland. She turned up the volume and sang, uninhibited, inside the dark-tinted windows; bought thickshakes from the highway drive-throughs and threw the empty cups on the passenger-side floor.

She arrived a little earlier than she had expected on a sunny afternoon following a morning of rain. Nobody was home and the daisy-spattered back lawn was steaming. Justine left her high heels on the porch and jumped off the edge, plunging her feet into the breathing green. Sherry woke from her old-dog dreams under the apple tree and shambled over to be patted. Justine caressed the soft fur at the old collie's throat and remembered how she was as a pup, setting and stalking before making a mad barking dash at kids running through sprinklers. It made her think of the paddling pool that was probably lying, deflated, under the house, and of little fat hands sticky from the meltings of red icypoles. She crouched down and spoke to the dog in a playful growl. Sherry did her arthritic best to answer the challenge, hunkering down into the set pose, elbows on the ground. Then Justine wrestled her to the ground, where they were both content to lie, for a moment, panting in the sun.

When she got too hot Justine retreated to the porch, brushing ineffectually at the grass stains on her cream linen pants. She peered down through the trees to the bottom of the garden and saw that her father had taken down the old swing set that had been a present for her fourth birthday, and planted out a vegetable garden in its place. It made her feel partially erased. But she was pleased to see her oldest boots, their leather bleached and cracked, still in the tumble of outdoor shoes beside the back door. She was sure they were hers. Until she put them on and felt how they slopped around on her feet, their elastic sides not even close to hugging her ankles. Stay-at-home Jill must have had a pair exactly the same. And Justine's own boots must, after all, have been thrown away.

Henri came home from overseas with a large white box tied up with pale blue ribbon.

'I think it's time we had a party,' he said, placing the box on the bed and kissing her neck as she unravelled the loops and bows. She threw open the lid of the box to find a party dress in the same dainty pearlescent blue as the ribbon.

'Oh,' she said, lifting the perfectly folded dress out of its box by its shoulders and holding it against her body while her mirror-self did the same.

'Oh,' she said.

'You like it then?'

'Oh, Henri.'

She loved the length and the shape of the sleeves, the neckline and gently tapered waist. She loved the name on the label; a name she had only ever seen written in the pages of the most expensive of fashion magazines and had no idea how to pronounce. She loved every single thing about the dress, except: 'I'm not going to be able to fill these out,' she said, despondently, once she had calculated the amount of bosom required by the gathering at the bodice.

'When will you learn to trust me?' Henri asked.

Justine took off her clothes and stepped into the watery cool of the pale blue silk, expecting to be disappointed by puckers in unfulfilled fabric. But as Henri manoeuvred the zip up the length of her back, she felt her breasts bloom into the softly gathered cups.

On the night of the party, it was as if the house had dressed up too, and it felt to Justine slightly strange, slightly remote, as if she were seeing it for the first time in a tuxedo and starched shirt. She had that special, but faintly useless, feeling in her own body, too; her newly polished fingernails too easily spoiled to touch things, her coiffure too unsteady to move her head too far to either side. She didn't know where to put her hands, or indeed herself, as Henri's guests began, in the early evening, to arrive.

The women were not young, but they were beautiful and dressed to be stroked in furs and feathers. The men guided their women through the hallways firmly, with fat and signet-ringed hands. For a laugh, Henri had brought the mannequins down from the attic. He had put them together with mix-and-match limbs, and found wigs only for some. But they were each dressed in party frocks — of indigo, scarlet, saffron, aquamarine — that were nearly as beautiful as Justine's own. On plaster-cast forearms Henri had balanced the caterer's platters. Some of the mannequins stood in corners, or within the frames of French windows, offering up the delicate nibbles; others were stationed beside linen-draped tables, gesturing invitingly towards sparkling forests of brimming champagne flutes.

Justine stood at the edge of a group of guests, listening, waiting for any of the speakers to join her to the conversation — by way of eye contact, at least. But with their glances they made a spider's web, and Justine could only watch it grow in complexity with each fresh exchange. She drifted away and tried several other groups, hovering on their peripheries until the embarrassment of her apparent insignificance became unbearable. She looked over to where Henri held court, his chest proud and puffed and covered by a waistcoat of the same claret colour as the fluid in his glass, but she did not want to go and simper at his side. She would show him that she could manage, that she could make herself useful. And so she went into the kitchen and took the plastic film from the top of a fresh platter of hors d'oeuvres.

She moved, purposefully now, between conversations, platter in hand, but the guests either waved her away as if she were an insect, or seemed not to see her at all. She made two complete circuits of the rooms into which the party had spread before giving up. She leaned on the wall just to one side of the open fire and popped a shrimp into her mouth, bursting its curled body between her teeth. Henri was looking at her from across the room, and suddenly she understood exactly what it meant to be caught in someone's gaze. She felt herself to be held there for a moment, trapped. Then she was released, Henri's eyes travelling to the ebony-skinned mannequin, who was bald but dressed in scarlet, standing with a plate of cheeses in her arms. He smiled and flicked his eyes back again to where Justine stood, identically posed. His smile broadened and she felt, first in her neck, and then simultaneously in her elbows and her knees, a stiffness that was creeping, seizing, cramping, aching. Before it reached her feet, her hands, Justine dropped the platter and ran. For the door. For her life.

Justine is living at home again now. Most evenings Jill brings home movies from the shop for Justine to watch, but she's seen everything in stock. In the afternoons their mother tucks a crocheted blanket around Justine's immobile legs and wheels her out onto the porch. Justine hates it, the horrible parody of it, her mother sitting with her as if she were a toddler, turning the pages of picture books prescribed by the woman from the rehab clinic.

'Say "duck" darling,' her mother says, pointing. 'D-uck.'

'Uck.'

'Like this, love: d-uck.'

'Uck.'

'Not quite, sweetie. D-uck.'

When Justine gets tired, her eyelids fall closed with a faint click.

'Don't get frustrated, lovey. I know you're trying. You're improving so much. Just have one more go and then we'll give it a rest. Have a try. D-uck.'

'Daaaaa-ck.'

'Oh, clever girl! Well done. That's right. Duck. Oh, you're doing so well.'

This is what her mother says, but Justine can see her wondering how it is that they have been so reduced, down to words of one syllable. And Justine has no means by which she might explain.

She had been found early in the morning after the party, face down in a garden bed freshly planted out with pansies, less than two blocks from Henri's house. In the days that followed, the owners of the pansies told her mother their side of things, a hundred times.

'I said don't touch her,' the woman said. 'I said that's the way you get stuck with a needle. I thought she was a druggie, you see. But he doesn't listen to me.'

'I thought it was too late,' the man said. 'When I put my hand on her arm she was all hard and cold. I rolled her over and she was stiff as a board.'

'Then I had a good look at the dress,' the woman said. 'And I knew she must have come from a good home.'

Even now, two years later, Justine holds the same pose, both arms bent ninety degrees, the fingers of each hand locked together in neat salutes. And still the doctors stick to their story and call it a stroke. They just ignore the things that don't make sense. Like the almost synthetic texture of Justine's hair, which no longer seems to grow. And the fact that her feet, two sizes smaller than they were when she left home, are arched and angled downwards, toes crimped together and pointed, as if in permanent acceptance of a high-heeled shoe.

ART

$\mathcal{E}den$

On the first day, Eve began. Well, it wasn't actually the first day. It had been four and a half weeks since they moved, but she had needed that time. She deserved a little holiday, and boxes didn't just unpack themselves into a new house. But now that she felt rested, and everything had been put away, she was ready to begin.

First, she would need breakfast. She couldn't begin on an empty stomach. And since it was such a significant day, she felt, breakfast should be somewhat celebratory. One of the farewell presents from the girls in the office was an apron printed with a picture of Michelango's *David*. She put it on, wishing they could see her now: ducking out to the shed in her gumboots to get an egg from underneath one of her own hens. She made pancakes, stacked them with maple syrup and banana slices, and took her plate out onto the veranda.

It was on this veranda that Eve had fallen in love with the place. The real estate agent, a chestnut-haired woman whom Eve was fairly sure was on Valium, had brought them out onto it to show them the view. 'Paradise,' she had sighed, parking her tortoiseshell glasses on top of her head and gesturing to the thoroughly unexceptional rural scene before her. In one direction there were rugged-up horses in a field of apple-tree stumps, and in the other an orchard of gnarled trees that dropped economically unviable fruit onto the grass. But to Eve, it *was* Paradise, this old pickers' hut flaking its green paint into a valley an hour's drive from the city. She loved the ruffles of sweet william along the driveway and the letterbox that perched in the forked branches of an old peach tree. Inside, the hut was daggy and funny, with chequered linoleum lifting in all the corners and incongruous, ostentatious light fittings. But after the sale of the city apartment, they'd been able to buy it outright and still have enough left over to buy a nice car for Adam, to take the sting out of commuting.

It was still dark in the mornings when he came into the bedroom to bring Eve a cup of tea just before he left for work.

'Today's the day, hey?' he had said this morning, and kissed her cheek.

'Yep. Today. Today, I begin.'

Eve finished her pancakes and washed the dishes. In the shower, she shaved her legs and noticed that her toenails were quite long. When she got out, she trimmed them with clippers. Then filed them into a nice shape. And since they were such a nice shape, it seemed a shame not to paint them. And so she did, in a shade of polish called *Rose Madder Lake*, which was exactly the same name as that of pencil number twenty-one in her set of Derwent Watercolours. Rose Madder Lake. It really ought, Eve thought as she applied a second coat, to have been the name of a famous synchronised swimmer. She sat for a while with her feet in front of the fan heater. And smiled when she realised that she had just begun. No-one could say that she hadn't painted *anything* today.

On the second day, Eve decided, she would begin properly. But what to wear? Everyone knows that there is no sense beginning a new gym campaign without a series of new lycra outfits; or horse-riding without jodhpurs and a nice velvet hat; or ballet classes without pointe shoes and a tutu. And Eve knew that she could not begin, seriously and formally, as a painter until she was dressed as one.

She had given away all her office clothes as a kind of insurance against going back and this had left her with a wardrobe full of smart casuals and party clothes. Back when she was only a hobbyist, dabbling with her paints in the sunroom of the city apartment on weekends, she used to wear Adam's old T-shirts and track pants. And *they* wouldn't do anymore.

There was a small town about twenty winding kilometres away. It had suffered a fatal blow ten years back when the arse fell out of the apple industry, but was being kept on life support by the hippies who came in once or twice a week from their shacks in the hills. It had no bank or post office, but it did have a café that made reasonable chai, and an op shop. Eve calculated that she could be back home inside an hour and a half.

'Swednesday,' said some passing dreadlocks to Eve on the street outside the op shop.

'Sorry?'

'It's…Wednesday.'

'Oh?'

'Doesn't open till two on Wednesdays.'

Eve looked at her watch. It was only noon.

'Oh. *Two*? Thanks.'

So Eve sat on a lumpy leather couch by the café's blue velvet curtains, drinking chai, reading old copies of *Wellbeing* magazine and watching the op shop's door. It was not entirely unproductive time, however. She also thought some bitchy thoughts about the abstract paintings on the café walls; an activity that certainly counted towards artistic practice.

The op shop opened a little after two and smelled like a silverfish's banquet of polyester armpits, mould and inner soles. But on a rack in the back room, Eve found what she was looking for. It was the perfect painter's shirt: striped and collarless, the fabric worn through at the folded edges of the cuffs. Someone had already worn it for painting. Probably they had thrown it out because of its smattering of small, hardened circles of paint. These paint spots were mostly in earth colours, and in reds and yellows, which was a good sign, since these were the colours with which Eve herself felt most comfortable. In general she stayed away from the violets and the deeper, more aggressive of the blues.

At home, in front of the bathroom mirror, Eve tried on her purchases. She admired how the shirt fell off her shoulders but clung just nicely to the sides of her breasts. The timber handle of a fine brush speared her hair just above her ponytail, which was tied off with a purple scarf she had found in a basket by the op shop's cash register. The trousers were loose and navy blue, the clogs leather and well worn. She felt pleased. Her canvas was blank and Adam would be home in half an hour, but she looked every bit the artist, and that wasn't a bad start.

On the third day, Eve slept in. She woke to the digital clock blinking 10.37am and knew that she would have to begin without breakfast. She lumbered her easel out through the narrow kitchen door to the veranda and assembled all her paints and brushes on a conveniently deep windowsill. This is what she had imagined, the first time she had stood on this veranda: herself painting while her hens clucked encouragingly from the lawn below. She was only there a few moments, however, before it became quite clear that she would soon be too cold in her striped painter's shirt.

She took her easel back inside and set it down in the living room at an angle to the window that looked out over the orchard and some distant hills. Not that she was going to look at the view. But if she did happen to pause for a moment and look around, there would be a calming vista just over her shoulder. The window also delivered good natural light to the canvas she now placed on the easel, and to the spot on the table where she was about to set up a still life scene.

Eve had been envisaging the composition for weeks, collecting gradually the component parts. For the backdrop, a square of chocolate velvet, scrunched into soft mountains to draw the eye up valleys and along ridges to the centre of the picture. Slightly to the left of centre would be a pewter pitcher, dull and bulbous as an atom bomb against the fabric. Clustering at the pitcher's base would be the fruit. There would be three apples, the first of them pinkish-red, a colossal Fuji, perfect and round as a Japanese valentine; the second, golden-skinned and tapered like a tooth. The third would bring the other two together, marry them in its bright stripes of red, orange and yellow. Called a Cox's Orange Pippin and collected as a windfall from the neighbouring orchard, it was a low, squat apple with a deep dimple for its stem. The solitary pear would sit, upright, to the left, keeping a respectful distance from the pitcher and the family of apples. But when Eve assembled the scene, just as she had imagined it, she saw immediately that there was a problem with the pear.

The pear was all wrong. One of the smooth, brown-skinned varieties of pear, it sat over to one side looking — in comparison with the vibrant apples — two dimensional and lifeless. Brown on brown just didn't work. What was needed, clearly, was a green pear. A fresh pear. A knobbly pear. One that would stand up for itself with its bright waxy skin, with bumps like hard, misplaced buttocks and breasts. Eve looked at her watch. She could make it to town and back in an hour and a half. Tops. Two if she had a quick bite of lunch while she was there.

When she returned, Eve picked out the greenest and knobbliest of the pears in a kilo bag and rested it on its base a few inches from the pewter pitcher. She stood back, by her easel, upon which her canvas was stretched. And blank. She observed her still life study in the centre of the table. The colours harmonised, the composition was in perfect balance. It was just right. It was five o'clock.

On the fourth day, Eve sat at her easel. She got up and walked around the room. She sat at her easel. She got up and made herself a cup of tea. Herbal. She sat at her easel. She sighed. Her tin of Derwent Watercolour pencils caught her eye. It had been months since she last used them, and when she opened the tin and lifted out the top tray she could see immediately that the pencils were out of order. She emptied them onto the table beside the still life ensemble and sorted them by number until she had a pleasing rainbow where there had been a jumble of shades. Some of her colours — number sixty-two, Burnt Sienna, and number fifty-six, Raw Umber — were now down to half-size. Others — like number thirty-seven, Oriental Blue, and number twenty-three, Imperial Purple — were still as tall as they were when brand-new. But even many of the lesser-used ones were quite blunt. And so she took up her metal pencil sharpener and began. At number one, Zinc Yellow.

She was up to number forty-one, Jade Green, when she heard the sound of a car in the driveway. Through the window she saw coming to a standstill the decrepit red mini with a stoved-in driver's side door that belonged to her friend Rosie. (Yes, that would be me, having made the difficult decision to cut Friday's media ethics lecture in favour of a drive in the country. She watched as I crawled out of the passenger-side door and hefted a wicker picnic basket — its gingham-covered lid concealing two bottles of cheap plonk — out of the back seat.)

'Rosie…' she started.

'Don't look at me like that. You can stop long enough to eat lunch.'

'*Lunch*?'

'Evie, it's one thirty.'

Eve took the basket, carried it into the house and placed it on the table where she thought it might conceal the pile of shavings edged with every colour of two-thirds of a rainbow. No such luck.

'I…um,' Eve said, trying to conjure up a justification.

'Oh dear. That bad?'

On the fifth day, Eve lost her confidence in the Cox's Orange Pippin. What she had wanted for the apple occupying that position in her painting — what she had seen when she had dreamed it — was the kind of luminous apple painted by Lucas Cranach the Elder in the tree above the auburn heads of his *Adam and Eve*.

Eve could picture almost every detail of the Cranach in her mind. She could conjure Eve's naked body, lumpy as her own knobbled pear. She could see Adam's befuddled scratching of his head, the zoo of placid animals at his feet and the serpent bending into a reverse S against the tree trunk. But although she could remember the apples bursting like stars all over the canopy of leaves, and although she could remember their gorgeous shades of gold and blood orange, she could not recall whether or not they had stripes. She flicked in her mind's eye between competing versions of the image. Striped apples, plain apples, striped apples, plain apples. Striped. Plain. The authentic version would not declare itself.

Somewhere in her bookshelf, Eve knew, she would have a reproduction. Somewhere in one of the expensive art history volumes she had failed to resist in the bookshop next door to her old office, there would be a reproduction of the Cranach to answer the riddle and determine the fate of the Cox's Orange Pippin.

She pulled down book after book, looking in their indexes. Cézanne, Chagall, Constable…Degas. Not trusting the apparent omission, she leafed through each book, page by careful page. It was lunchtime when Adam came in from the shed to find her sitting, disconsolate, in a puddle of splayed books.

'Come on, Evie,' he said. 'Give it a rest now.'

On the sixth day, it was Sunday, and that was a good enough excuse.

On the seventh day, by mid-morning, Eve had almost finished. She was up to number sixty-six, Chocolate. She had not intended, on this day, to touch the pencils. In fact, she had strictly forbidden herself any more sharpening. But then she realised that if she finished sharpening all of the pencils, it would offer up some kind of proof that she was capable of finishing things. And as soon as she had finished the pencils, she could begin painting.

When she heard a knock at the door, Eve decided not to answer it. Whoever it was could go away. She picked up pencil number sixty-seven, Ivory Black, and inserted it in the sharpener. Then a face moved into the frame of the window. The man belonging to the face had wild, windblown hair and wore a checked scarf knotted tightly around his neck. The hand he held in the air, which was about to knock on the window, turned from a rapping fist into a coy little wave. The only reason Eve opened the door was to go outside and shout at him.

'Who the fuck are you?'

He hunched himself apologetically.

'I am ever so sorry…'

'If I had wanted to talk to you, I would have opened the door. Now fuck off.'

He appeared not to notice her displeasure. He was smiling and nodding, as if in assent. She could see the monolithic white teeth in his wide mouth, which sat above a goatee and a nose that one might describe as…well, how would one describe his nose?

A Word from Rosie Little
ON WRITING ABOUT NOSES

I could get all writerly about it, and call it an 'aquiline nose', but to do so would be to confine its owner for all time to the pages of fiction, for how could I ever expect you to believe that he truly existed if I were to plonk such a literary phenomenon squarely in the middle of his face? An actual nose — a nose of flesh and bone and cartilage — might in fact *be* aquiline in profile, but it is a strange fact of life that it is almost never so described unless the describer has a pen in her hand or a keyboard beneath her fingertips.

I cannot account for the magnetism that so routinely brings the words 'aquiline' and 'nose' end to end in the midst of a writer's description of a face. But I have been told that in the French language, the two halves of *nez aquilin* are so rarely separated that to spy any other word cosying up to *aquilin* would be akin to witnessing an infidelity. It just seems to be a fact of linguistic life, as obvious as the proverbial, that 'aquiline' has a peculiar adjectival jurisdiction when it comes to the literary rendering of the olfactory organ. And so, numbered among the great aquiline noses of literary history, are those of Bram Stoker's Count Dracula (and at least two of his vampiric consorts), Peter Carey's Harry Joy, the doctor (but only the doctor?) in Mario Vargas Llosa's *Aunt Julia and the Scriptwriter* and Monsieur de Rênal, the mayor of Vérrieres in Stendhal's *The Red and the Black.* Anton Chekov was fond of the aquiline nose, giving one to a doctor and one to a professor who appear in his short stories. George Eliot may even have had an aquiline nose complex, given that she put one in Chapter 21 of *Adam Bede*, one in Chapter 58 of *Middlemarch* and one in Chapter 7 of *The Mill on the Floss*. I could keep going, of course, but I would begin to bore you. Instead, I shall prove my point by leaving you some space to jot down the next five aquiline noses that you encounter in your reading career, and betting that it won't be very long until they're all filled:

Aquiline Nose 1. _____

Aquiline Nose 2. _____

Aquiline Nose 3. _____

Aquiline Nose 4. _____

Aquiline Nose 5. _____

But what precisely does an aquiline nose look like? I am certain that I read and envisaged a great many before I ever bothered to find out. 'Aquiline', to me, had always suggested something watery; the kind of long, thin nose given to unfortunate dripping. When in fact, I have lately discovered, it is

curved like the beak of an eagle and indicates
— to some psychic face-readers at least — a
strong will, independence and the promise of
prosperous mid-years.

*

'Well go away then.'

'Yes, yes.'

'You're not going.'

'Yes indeed. I have something for you, you see.'

Eve noticed the convertible near her peach tree letterbox, and thought it unlikely that he was delivering parcels for Australia Post.

'Are you a salesman?'

'May I come inside? I find this winter of yours very cold.'

'You are a salesman.'

'Salesman. Such an unattractive word, don't you think?'

'Right. I'm not interested, thanks. I've got work to do. So if you don't mind — goodbye.'

'But I do have something for you,' he said.

'You're still not going. Go on. Off you go.'

'You don't want then, to see a reproduction of the Cranach?'

'Is this a joke?'

'You are Eve?'

'Did someone get you to come here for a joke? Do you work with Adam? Are you from some radio station?'

'No, no, but all reasonable suspicions, for I see I have hit the nail on the head. But it's no practical joke. It's obvious, my dear. Here you are, an artist in an apple grove. Of course you would be looking for the Cranach. Of course you should paint apple trees, and apples. Small red apples with sweet snow-white insides, the big green globes of the Cleos, the carnival stripes of the Cox's Orange Pippin. Yes, especially those. Apples are your calling. It doesn't take a genius to see that.'

'Well, show me then.'

He gestured to gathering storm clouds.

'All right then. Just for a minute though. And I'm not buying anything, okay? Are you clear on that?'

'Quite.'

'Absolutely clear?'

'*Absolutement*,' he said, handing Eve an embossed postcard.

The Art of the World, in seven slender volumes bound in ivory leather, is the ideal accompaniment to the *Encyclopaedia Atlantica*. Do you have an interest in a particular artist? The *Encyclopaedia Atlantica* will provide you with in-depth information about the life and times of the artist, as well as an understanding of their place in history. But only *The Art of the World* can show you, in first-class colour reproduction, the works which earned them that place in the pages of the most respected encyclopaedia in the world.

'Drivel,' the salesman said.

'Pardon?'

'Drivel, don't you think? Now I — I would never insult you with such pedestrian prose.'

He fanned the seven pristine volumes across Eve's table like a card sharp fans a deck.

'Think of a painting, any painting,' he dared her.

'I just want to see the Cranach.'

'Please. Think of any painting. Any painter. Any period. I think I may prove to you that any painting you desire to see before your eyes is here, within these pages.'

'I told you I wasn't buying anything, so you're wasting your time.'

'Time, I have plenty of. Think. Allow a painting to take shape in your mind. And I shall show it to you.'

She thought. Of the Cranach.

'Come, now. That's hardly a challenge. I already know you want to see that. Now think of something else.'

It was a nude. Titian's *Venus of Urbino*, lying langorously upon a bed of cushions. Eve tried to think instead of the *Mona Lisa*. The Titian was too sexy; he might take it as a come-on. And besides, he'd never guess anything as obvious as the da Vinci. But still, the irrepressible nude pushed to the forefront of Eve's mind.

His hand passed over the fan of books like a magician's. He selected a volume. The pages fluttered and then the book fell open in his hands.

'Ah, Titian. He was very great, Titian, was he not? There was a limerick — rather blue, I'm afraid:

> *As Titian was mixing rose madder,*
> *his model reclined on a ladder.*

Her position, to Titian,
suggested coition,
so he climbed up the ladder and had her.

Quite good, don't you think?'

Eve was silent, blanched.

'I do hope I've not offended.'

Eve thought of Chagall's brides and grooms floating through the air past weeping candelabras, of Kahlo's face beneath the antlers of a deer, of an apple tree by Klimt. And each the encyclopaedia salesman was able to produce, there upon the page.

'I have proved myself to you, no? Shall you take a set, young Eve? A valuable addition to the library of any young artist. Surely you agree?'

'I'm not an artist. My *father* is an artist. I just sharpen pencils.'

'Now that cannot be true. I see you have your still life assembled here. A sensible place to begin. Let me see your canvas.'

The encylopaedia salesman slid past her.

'Ah, I see,' he said, registering the blankness. 'Perhaps I can help.'

He took up a palette and oozed several bright worms of paint onto its smeared surface. He handed it to her, placed a brush in her hand.

'Paint.'

'I can't — this is ridiculous.'

'Paint!'

'I can't just...*paint*.'

'Paint. Just paint what you see.'

She stood before her easel, and lifted the brush.

'I can't. I can't do this.'

'I think you'll find that you can.'

And then the brush, seemingly of its own accord, plunged towards the palette. And Eve began to paint. Slowly at first, as if the air around her was too thick. Then faster, the brush moving between canvas and palette, seeming to pick and mix colours all by itself. It carried her hand behind its hovering point, touching deftly to the canvas, tracking in perfect arcs with this colour, then that. So subtle. Appearing before her was her own vision. What she saw in her mind's eye was transporting itself to the canvas through the conduit of the brush. No sooner did the paint touch the canvas than it was dry and ready to receive the next layer. The brush picked up yet more speed, towing streaks of paint away from the centre in broad, brave strokes. Apples filled out and ripened on the canvas before her. The flow of the paint was positively ecstatic. She painted and painted, and oh! painted. And then the brush stopped, stalling in her hand, its tip just millimetres from the surface. The painting, Eve could see, was one leaf-green brushstroke from finished. But the brush would not move. Even though completion was so close. She was so on the brink. It was unbearable. It could not possibly. Stop.

'*Cherie*, one thing first. Sign here.'

In place of the brush, he placed a pen, and she dashed off

her signature before grabbing back the brush, which applied itself, with a final flourish, to the dainty, curling leaf. And then Eve felt herself fainting. She was falling, falling. And the last thing she saw before the blackness was his smile, its colossal white teeth and, between them, flicking quick as whiplash, a forked tongue.

'*Au revoir, cherie*,' said the encyclopaedia salesman to the unconscious Eve, who had fallen — her hair streaked carmine, viridian, sulphurous yellow — across the table next to her fruits. Which were almost undisturbed. Only the pear had rolled onto its knobbled side.

When she came to, Eve found her house empty of the seller of the *Encyclopaedia Atlantica* and other fine publications. But her painting — her painting! — was still there. And it was beautiful. It was the most beautiful thing she had ever painted. It was a painting of dream apples, and it was perfect. Except for one small thing. She looked at the Cox's Orange Pippin in the painting. On the skin of its curving edge there was a mark. She looked at its model, the apple upon the table. But it was untouched. She moved closer to the canvas, peering into the structure of the paint itself. Adjusting her focus she saw it, in the striped skin of the painted apple: a set of teeth marks surrounding a sickle of sweet, white flesh.

LOVE

The Anatomy of Wolves

THE WOLF HAS LEGS.

A nd these were the parts of him that I saw first. I was standing at the bottom of a backstage staircase and he was standing at the top, his hairy shins and Blundstone boots sticking out from beneath the hem of a taffeta ballgown in an alarming shade of yellow, his hair cropped close for a soldier's part.

'You must be Reporter Rosie,' he said, and I liked the sound of his voice.

'Is now a good time?'

'Rehearsals start again at two, so we could do it over lunch, if you like,' he said.

'Only if you leave that dress on. And promise not to say "eclectic".'

'What?'

'Eclectic. If you say the word eclectic then I shall be forced to hate you and write evil things about your play,' I said, brandishing notebook and pen.

'In which case, I forswear all words beginning with "e".

From now until we have finished our fish and chips.'

At least, I think that is what we said. We were, after all, of an age when first conversations are frequently blurred by the static of the subtext. I was twenty-two and only just beginning to acknowledge my transformation from painfully skinny to quite acceptably thin. However, I was yet to discover that the girls I went to school with — the ones who had been so enamoured of their various swellings — were now beginning to worry that their bodies' expansionist programs knew no bounds.

I had graduated from university and begun work. Cured of my adolescent desire for Latin terms, I embarked on my career ready to treat words with the no-nonsense discipline they deserved. I had read my George Orwell. And so, on the day I went down the coast to the city to begin my cadetship at the slightly less well regarded of the two metropolitan daily news-papers, I knew that I wouldn't be the type to write 'commence' when what I really meant to say was 'start'.

I would not let Latinate terms fall on the facts like snow. No, my words would be as blunt as clubs made from the timber of good, solid Anglo-Saxon tree trunks.

I became the arts reporter. But you should not imagine that my job was glamorous. Those just ahead of me had progressed to more prestigious rounds such as Special Correspondent for Chrysanthemum Shows or Chief Animal Story Reporter. And believe me, those on the animal beat got a lot more front pages than I did. Many of the early days of my working life were spent interviewing earnest young musicians who wore black and said 'eclectic'.

'Our style is really, um, eclectic. We don't like to categorise ourselves,' they said. They all said, five minutes before they lay down on the ground and were photographed from above with their heads in daisy formation, and a few hours before they taped their set lists to their amps and launched into a night of tuneless covers. For a while, I put a dollar in a tin on my desk every time I heard the word eclectic. Within a couple of years, I was fairly certain, I'd be able to buy a car with the proceeds. Trade in the Mini on something with more cachet: a little old Triumph Spitfire or a Fiat Bambino. But about three weeks later, when the tin contained twenty-seven dollar coins, I bought a pair of strappy red velvet heels that were on sale, but which I never could wear because when I stood up in them my toenails went black from the pressure (the Shoe Goddess, presumably, was on leave).

But all of this is to one side of the point, which is, as I'm sure you've divined, that I did interview the actor in his yellow ballgown, over a lunch of fish and chips, during which he only once slipped up on his solemn oath (an 'emotion' sneaking into one of his sentences), and by the end (he would have said 'conclusion') of which, I was almost certainly in love.

THE WOLF HAS A TONGUE.

At the party on the opening night of the play, he licked my ear.

'You smell of raspberries,' he said.

'Strawberries,' I corrected.

It was the perfume I always wore.

'Whatever. It's definitely edible.'

'Careful. That's an "e" word.'

But when he took me home to his bed in his Boys' Own Adventure share house, there were no more words. In that den-smelling room, licking turned into nipping turned into sucking and biting. We were young and playful animals, rough and tumbling. We were roly-poly cubs. Afterwards, we had a shower together in the dark. Hot water stung on grazed and tingling skin, and I remember breathing steam into which, it seemed, had been dissolved the very essence of him.

We returned to his bed and stayed there all through the heat of the day, listless as midday lions for the most part, but rousing ourselves occasionally for the purpose of consuming food, or each other. In the evening, I walked with him to the theatre and, at the stage door, offered up my tongue for him to swallow.

'Good luck for the show,' I said when we pulled ourselves apart, just before I remembered that this was not the thing to say at all.

A Word from Rosie Little
ON THEATRICAL TRADITIONS

Whistling backstage, the naming of the Scottish play, the wishing of good luck: all these things are forbidden in the theatre. Instead of 'good luck', one might of course say 'break a leg', a saying that may or may not, once upon a time, have referred to the hope that an actor's performance would be so good that when it was over, s/he would have to 'break' the line of his/her leg in the action of bowing, or in bending down to pick up coins from the stage. Alternatively, it may or may not refer back to the actual leg of John Wilkes Booth, which was *literally* fractured in 1865 when Booth leapt up onto a stage while attempting to escape after having assassinated Abe Lincoln.

But there is another traditional alternative to 'good luck'; one that I have recently learned, and one that would — in hindsight at least — have been eerily apt in the circumstances in which I found myself outside the stage door that evening. *In bocca al lupo*, I might have said. *Into the mouth of the wolf.* It's an Italian phrase that is meant to bestow luck and instil courage, and it is properly answered *crepi il lupo: I shall eat the wolf.*

*

THE WOLF HAS A STOMACH.

Only weeks later, we moved in together, renting a small flat behind a pizza shop, although this did not prevent us from ringing up to order home deliveries. In those early months, we played house like newlyweds, learning to make apricot chicken from the recipe on the back of the French onion soup packet and buying white goods from garage sales. Each payday we got something new from the supermarket: a peeler, a potato masher or a whisk. Once the kitchen cupboards and drawers were full, we were at a loss, so we made ourselves into a nuclear family with a tabby from the cat shelter. We called her Gelfling and smiled, indulgent as fond parents, while she frayed our furniture and tortured lizards on the front step.

THE WOLF HAS EYES.

They were big and green and sad — set deeply in the kind of strong-boned face Laurence Olivier wore to play Heathcliff — and when I met his mother, I found out where they were from. Hers, however, seemed even bigger and sadder because they lived in a tiny heart-shaped face that looked as if it were crafted from some sort of flesh-coloured putty. The jaw and the brow, it seemed, had come from his father: a priest with a limp. His parents, he told me, had come together out of childhoods full of alcohol and violence. Through good works, he said, they were determined to repair the damage. They didn't approve of us living together, but since they were proper Christians and did not judge, we were invited as a couple to the family home for dinner. I wore a nice blouse and my hair neatly brushed and took my place at a table that was extended and set with plastic salt and pepper shakers which, when set together, formed a pair of hands in prayer. There were wineglasses on the table and his father filled them from a carafe of diluted orange juice. We bowed our heads while one of the foster children said a simple grace. The other — little more than a toddler, I was told —

was in a bedroom beating his head against a wall that he had already smeared with his own shit. Through two closed doors we could hear the banging as well as a noise that sounded like the screaming of a trapped rabbit.

'I don't know if I'll ever crack that one,' said his mother, looking sad.

THE WOLF HAS CLAWS.

But I didn't see them for quite a long time. There were too many diversions. Often, he did the housework as Jesus, wrapped in a white sheet and singing Sunday school hymns over the top of the howling industrial vacuum cleaner that we borrowed once a fortnight or so from the pizza shop. He was ecumenical, though. Sometimes the sheet was orange and he chanted faux-Buddhist mantras as he scrubbed the shower and the loo. Once, when I was sick with a cold, he borrowed a nurse's outfit from the theatre's costume hire shop, and ministered to me in a lispy falsetto until I laughed myself better.

In the name of cheap fun, we sprayed our hair silver and bought old-people's clothes from the Salvos. He in a stinky, crumpled suit, and me in a lavender print frock and fake pearls, staggered theatrically on walking sticks through the car yards of the city asking to test drive the motors of any salesmen we judged to be too inexperienced or too superstitious to tell us to get lost. For the winter solstice we took blankets and candles to the local cemetery and read vampire stories to each other while the concrete cold of the graves seeped into our bones through our bums.

More and more often, though, we stayed home at night on the weekends and watched old movies on video. We told ourselves that we were compiling a history of our culture. We stopped cooking and lived on Hawaiian pizzas and on the rolls of garlic bread that would otherwise have been chucked in the pizza shop's bin. We slept late, always on the weekends and often on weekdays too, Gelfling purring between us.

I brought home two copies of the newspaper each evening to avoid fights over who got to do the crossword puzzle. We folded into each other like a pair of socks.

I remember the night of his birthday in colours. There was the beetle-green glitter in Cleopatra-tapers on the eyelids of one of the girls from the theatre crowd, and the peacock silk shirt of a guy with a mass of salty-white hair. There was the red of my brief tartan skirt, beneath which my knickers showed each time I leaned over the pool table to take a shot, and the swirls and layers of bright liquor that were poured into shot glasses as we competed to drink more, and in stranger combinations, from the top shelf. The music was loud and silly, but with an irresistible dance-about beat. I got drunk. We all did. I was heady, giggly and high. And then, suddenly, alone.

'Oh yeah,' said the Cleopatra girl, lining up the black. 'He went home.'

Cross and confused, I walked the few blocks to our flat without a coat, the cold of the night bringing a kind of sobriety. When I got there, he was sitting in the dark. The light I switched on was bright and I saw that he had been crying. The rims of his eyes were stretched and reddened. He looked as if he had been poisoned, his irises a malignant green, his lips and cheeks pale and slack. But I was not sensible enough to be afraid.

He shouted and accused.

'Why didn't you just fuck him?'

'Who?'

'Why didn't you just get up on the pool table and spread your legs for him?'

'You're not making any sense,' I said, shouting too.

He stood over me, but I did not back down. Nor did I see it coming. It was too far beyond my experience, too far outside my expectations. His fist felt huge against my small face.

On the couch, I couldn't sleep. In our bed, he could. In the early hours of the morning I was still awake, stunned and pressing a packet of frozen peas to my cheek, when he briefly woke and stumbled into the living room. He was disoriented, and did not seem to see me. I watched in the darkness as he took aim and pissed all over the television set, then took himself back to bed.

When the true morning came I woke from an uncomfortable half-sleep clutching a warm bag of squashed peas. He was squatting by the television, dressed neither as Jesus nor a monk, but looking penitent anyway with a bucket of soapy water and a sponge. He saw that I was awake, but said nothing; just went on cleaning and wiping and dusting, in the living room, the kitchen and the bathroom, while I watched from my couch-island in silence. When the house was clean, he shaved and showered and dressed a little more neatly than was usual. On his way out the door, he kissed my cheek softly and I smelled shampoo in the wet flick of his hair against my nose.

He came home with treats, and to begin with I was like a child who would not be enticed. I shook my head to chocolates in the shape of ladybirds wrapped in shiny red foil and to a tiny iridescent fish in a plastic bag of water. I cried and said no to striped socks with toes in them and to a jar full of tiny rubber dinosaurs that were purple, orange and yellow. But I caved in when he ran me a bath and filled it with bubbles from a bottle that looked like a magnum of champagne. I let him put a cotton pad soaked in witch-hazel over my bruised and swollen eye, and read to me — doing all the voices and accents, too — from *The Snow Goose*, which made me cry. He put me to bed in clean sheets and got in beside me, and I kept crying while he kissed every part of me, and the tears were a drug whose effect felt strongly like love.

I slept all day and, when I woke up, there was pizza for dinner and *National Velvet* on the video.

'Come on the Pie,' he said, in perfect mimicry of little Lizzie Taylor, and I laughed. There had been some kind of aberration, but reality, it seemed, had now been restored. The next day, at a pharmacy in a suburb where I would never normally shop, I bought the kind of make-up that older women wear to give them 'more coverage'. I wore it for a week, and then life went on as before.

THE WOLF HAS FUR.

When I first met him it had been clipped close to the scalp, but by the time we had been living together for nine months it was brushing the collar of his shirt. It was very dark, with a patch of bright white in the back where, he said, it had lost its memory. It was soft and glossy and I loved to fiddle with it while we were watching television and sculpt it into devil's horns when it was full of shampoo in the bath. Over the winter, I took an impressive lead in the all-time Scrabble match tally that we kept in permanent texta down the side of our fridge, and he threatened to cut his hair unless I agreed to a ban on the tricky two-letter words that were the centrepiece of my strategy. Within a month, we were back to level-pegging.

The morning after the night on which he hit me for the second time, he looked at my face and then he put his head in my lap and cried. I stroked and soothed him, pushing my fingers into the dense, dark pelt of his beautiful hair. The grazed skin on the inside of my mouth felt, to my tongue's touch, like raw steak. I could still taste blood.

I had been late home from work. I could claim no big story, no pressing deadline — only a need to catch up on all the mornings lost to late sleeping and extended lunch hours spent going home to him. I had arrived to find the flat in darkness and full of the sweet smell of crushed juniper berries. I flicked on the light and saw the unhidden evidence of the empty gin bottle.

I let some light into the black bedroom along with myself, but he was not in the bed. He was crouched in the corner, a foetal shape, just the outline of him and his shaggy head picked out by the scattered motes of light.

'I thought you'd left me,' he said. A whimper.

I crouched down beside him, held out the back of my hand as if to a wounded dog.

'Hey, I was just at work. I'm sorry, I should have called.'

'You'll leave me. One of these days you'll leave me, I know you will,' he said, louder now.

'I won't. I won't. I won't ever leave you.'

'Don't LIE,' he snarled, a fist striking out of his dark hunch.

Later that week, my bruises under the cover of the older women's make-up, we sat at his parents' table while the only foster child in the house said grace. The head-banging one had gone to live somewhere else. We all said amen into our laps and then the house resumed a silence that didn't feel safe. For all of the time it had taken her to make the gravy, his mother had said nothing. Now she pushed some food onto her fork and brought it halfway to her mouth, then put it down again as if it disgusted her. She looked up at her son with her big and green and sad eyes.

'Did you do that to her?'

'What?'

'You did do that to her, didn't you?'

'Do what?'

'I know what it looks like when a man hits a woman. I know exactly what it looks like. And it looks like that.'

'Mum.'

'I can't. I just can't,' she said, standing up at the table and taking away his still-full plate and mine. She tipped our meat and vegetables into the pedal bin and let the lid fall. She was standing over it, sob-breathing and gulping, as we left the house. In the dark of the driveway, I felt ashamed.

THE WOLF HAS TEETH.

It was true that his top incisors sloped inward a little, making his canines appear quite prominent; but it was not these that bit. It was the clean and white-painted right angle of the edge of our bedroom door. I hammered into it fast, a dervish, whirling. My brow-bone fractured on impact. Skin split and out poured unexpectedly dark blood. It streaked down the white paint as I slid to the floor.

I had gone home, to my parents' house, for a weekend. I had rattled northwards, out of the city, in my little old Mini, but not without fear of what I would find when I returned. This time, it was tequila instead of gin. And this time, my hands were up, quickly, in a flimsy block between my face and his chest. I felt adrenalin gush to my hands and feet as he grabbed me, tightly, and held me by both wrists.

'Why did you even bother to come back?'

'I have no idea,' I screamed, my pulse hammering.

'You love them more than you've ever loved me.'

'Of course I do, you stupid fuck.'

He pulled me towards him and then pushed. I left his grip in a fast, hard spin, a dance move out of control, and collected the door with my face.

*

In the second moment of impact it was me that was stationary and the object that was moving. It was a needle, coming right towards my eye. Slowly, slowly, leaving plenty of time for the apprehension of pain.

'Close your eyes,' the nurse said from out of white space.

But I couldn't. I could only think of aqueous and vitreous humour, the liquid and the jelly that made my eyeball a globe, and how, if the needle slipped, they might leak out and my eyeball would be just a slimy white casing like a fish skin tossed in the scuppers.

It didn't slip. It just numbed my skin so that when the second needle came, towing its lengths of black thread, I could feel only the tugging as the nurse quilted the skin between my eyebrows. When he had finished, he let me sit up so I could look at myself in a mirror.

The wound would heal and, over time, fade into a pale crescent scar. One time, much later on, I would colour the moon-shaped mark blue and call myself a maiden of Avalon. But now it was an ugly gash of puckered skin and knotted twine marking the midpoint of eye sockets stained magenta and purple. My forehead was swollen and misshapen. The fine crack revealed by the X-ray was concealed beneath my swollen forehead, but in the mirror I could see the unmissable sign of ownership. A brand.

I was not allowed to leave the hospital until I had seen the domestic violence counsellor. She was not much older than I was, and her long hair was held back with a polka-dot bandana.

She wore her wrong-side-of-the-tracks accent like a badge of pride, saying 'arks' for 'ask' and 'was' for 'were'. But it was a dialect of blunt truth and I could not evade its meanings, no matter how delicately I danced around them with pretty words.

'He'll bash you again,' she said.

I argued that I knew how to avoid it now. If I could just keep my mouth shut at the right moment. If I didn't provoke him when he'd been drinking. She looked at me wearily, and I began to hear myself. After I had been silent for a time, she looked at her watch and said that I could go.

'You'll have to have someone pick you up, but. Your mum, maybe?'

I shook my head.

'Well, who was you going to call then?'

I didn't know. Beyond the yellowed curtain of the Emergency Department cubicle there were people milling about, but none of them belonged to me. I was alone. I had been delivered to the hospital by policemen (called to our house by the pizza cook), and one of them had sat in the back of the car with me and held his handkerchief to my bleeding face.

'Must be someone.'

There was only one person. I was cold and shivering and all I wanted was him. I wanted to kiss him on his lips, and then to drive my teeth into them, furious with love for him, and draw blood. But instead I took a taxi to the home of a friend who wouldn't scold.

In the late morning — washed, and dressed in borrowed clothes — I went back to the apartment behind the pizza shop.

He was sleeping. I sat beside him for a while, on the edge of our bed, watching dream-tremors flit through the muscles under the skin of his face. Gelfling, plump as a cushion in the crook of his knees, fixed me with one yellow and disdainful eye, as if she knew my decision already.

THE WOLF HAS A HEART.

And there were times, during the year of my lesson in wolf anatomy, when I was close enough to see it. Just a glimpse of it, beating red and slick inside the dark fur. I have to think hard, now, to remember how it looked. But I did see it. I'm sure that I did.

COMMITMENT

The Depthlessness of Soup

Sitting across the table from one another, at about ten past eight on the evening of the second anniversary of the day that they'd met, Paula and Will were like a pair of dangerously inflated balloons. Each of them had something important to say to the other, and the words that would make up these important somethings were already in their lungs, clinging like horseback riders to molecules of oxygen, impatiently awaiting a chance to escape. So preoccupied were Paula and Will by the sensation of mounting pressure within their chests that neither of them actually saw the waitress. The soup, a consommé, appeared simply to land — in wide, white bowls — on the table before them.

Perhaps it was the rising vapours of the soup that alerted the waiting words to the fact that an opportunity was nigh. Or perhaps it was the crusty warm scent of the bread rolls on the side plates. But in any case, by the time Paula and Will took up their spoons, words were jockeying in their mouths, swelling out their cheeks. Paula and Will each parted their lips in order to take a shallow sip of air, and the trapped and pent-up words took their chance, making a headlong, hurdy-gurdy rush for the big outside world.

The crucial question is, of course, whose words would get there first? But in order to answer this question, we must consider the events that took place in the lives of Paula and Will in the week leading up to the anniversary dinner, and also some elementary facts of physics.

1. What Will did in the week leading up to the anniversary
He took Wednesday afternoon off work and drove across town, through the industrial suburbs with their workshops and warehouses, to the home of Paula's father, who no longer lived with Paula's mother. She had quite dispassionately up and left him a few days after the youngest of their four daughters finished school, and then, once the paperwork was in order, married a quiet and gentle bachelor with notably short legs. Will thought it was rather as if she had simply decided that at her stage of life one was better off with a dachshund than an alsatian.

Paula's father was not the sort of man Will could ever imagine himself being able to hug, but he hoped to be able to conclude today's conversation with a warm handshake, perhaps even one of the sincere, two-handed variety. That's if Paula's father was at home. Will had decided not to ring first, because Paula's father might have asked what he wanted to see him about, and that would have been awkward. It was not a conversation he wanted to have over the phone.

The house was a charmless red brick square, out the front of which was a cemented yard with a few circular sinkholes that were home to straggly and untended rosebushes. Will didn't bother to ring the doorbell, just followed the sound of an idling engine around the side of the house to the garage in the backyard. Here Paula's father stood between the nostrils, and beneath the raised sky-blue hood, of his 1955 Holden FJ.

As he crossed the yard, Will felt in his pocket for the box containing the ring that he had on Monday collected from the jeweller. Paula's father wasn't exactly the type to appreciate the subtleties of the design, but a diamond that size was expensive in anyone's language. Will might not even show it, but it was there, as a prop, in case he needed a graphic demonstration of just how serious he was.

Standing a few metres behind Paula's dad, Will coughed, but not loudly enough to be heard over the engine. He coughed again, louder this time, but still Paula's father remained intent on the FJ's whirring mechanics. Will tuned in for a moment to the melody of the engine, and even he — who had scarcely more than a postage stamp's worth of knowledge on the subject of car engines — could tell that it was singing off-key. The irregular revs gathered into a crescendo. There was a muffled explosion, and then silence.

'You motherfucking cunt of a fucking pox-headed arse-wipe,' said Paula's father slowly, distributing his emphasis equally among the words.

Will coughed, audibly now, and the man to whom he was about to apply for the position of son-in-law turned around with a fierce sort of a look that changed to one of total incomprehension.

'Yes?' he asked.

Will coughed again, this time just to clear his throat.

'It's Will…just in case you, um…'

'Something I can do for you?'

'I, um…trouble with your car, I see.'

'No shit, Sherlock.'

Vigorously, Paula's father rubbed his filthy hands with an equally filthy rag.

'I wanted to talk to you about Paula.'

'Paula? Oh. Oh, right,' he said, and Will could have sworn that he heard the small ker-tish of a penny dropping.

Just as soon as the said unit of currency had landed, though, Paula's father tucked his rag into the pocket of his overalls and walked around to the side of the car and slid into the driver's seat.

'I'd like to marry her,' Will said, but the last half of his sentence was drowned in the ineffectual churning of the starter motor.

'What's that?' Paula's father called through the open car door, then turned the key and planted his foot again.

'I'd like to marry her!' Will said, trying to shout over the staggered bursts of mechanical noise.

The car fell silent and Paula's father hauled himself out from behind the wheel. Returning to the front of the car, he planted both hands on the edge of the engine well and peered into the workings.

'I'd like to marry her,' Will repeated, edging around to stand by the passenger-side headlight where he might catch the older man's eye.

'Fucking oath,' said Paula's father, but Will was almost certain that the curse pertained to the car and not to his inquiry.

'So, is it okay? If I marry her?'

'Who, Paula?'

'Yes.'

'What's it got to do with me?'

'Well, you know, traditionally...I thought it would be polite, you know, the done sort of thing, to come, and ask...'

'Been a long time since any of my bloody daughters listened to anything I had to say.'

'So it's okay with you then?'

Paula's father looked up from the engine and Will felt, for the first time since he'd arrived, that he had his full attention.

'Better ask Paula, mate. Reckon you'll find that she'll be the one to decide whether she's going to marry you or not.'

2. *What Paula did in the same week*

She booked in for Thursday, in her lunch hour, even though she knew the timing meant that until Saturday night she would have to take showers in private and keep her pants on whenever Will was around. It wasn't like they had sex every single night (they were past that stage) so she knew that she would manage to keep the surprise under wraps.

The salon was part of a day spa whose humid, below-ground premises smelled of chlorine and Epsom salts. Although the receptionist invited her to take a seat while she waited, Paula preferred to stand. As she stood, she conducted — by way of surreptitious glances into a mirrored wall — an honest appraisal of her physical self. Once she had pushed back her shoulders, dropped her chin slightly and tilted her pelvis to minimise the profile of her tummy, she was fairly content with the look of her body. She was slightly thick through the middle, but that was just the way she was made, and there was nothing more she could do about it than she already did at the gym twice a week. Her clothes were perfectly respectable: tailored, colour coordinated. Much less attention-seeking than the only other client in the waiting room, a skinny girl in chunky red boots that made her look like Olive Oyl. Paula was, she knew, a slightly unimaginative dresser, but she had some time ago accepted that she was simply not like the artists and designers at the advertising agency where she worked, who could afford to get around in hipster jeans and crushed shirts and blue hair. A good personal assistant wanted to exude control and efficiency, and Paula knew that she did just that.

Recognising the mental leap she had just made, from body and clothing to character and competency, she gave her reflected self a disapproving look. Precisely how short, she wondered, *was* the shortcut from the fit of one's skirt to the success of one's career? She had taken Gender Studies at university and ought, therefore, to have known better than to take that route, she chided herself. And then continued on with her appraisal, regardless. It was healthy, she thought, to be fully aware of one's own character traits, good and bad. She knew that her worst faults were irritability and a high susceptibility to PMT. But these weren't really such terrible flaws. Certainly not the sort of things that would prevent a man from wanting to marry you, for instance. Generally, she was very good-humoured; she was well organised, persistent and — somewhat incongruously with her conservative dress style, she liked to think — an energetic and uninhibited sexual partner. And it was this last segment of her personality that had brought her to the salon in the first place.

'It's Paula, is it?'

An elfin creature, her dead-straight hair coloured in several shades of pale blonde, padded across the tiles of the reception area in her tiny white-plush slippers.

'I'm Mary-Joy. This way, please,' she said, and Paula caught both the hint of an accent and the quick silver flash of a cross bouncing against Mary-Joy's tanned throat.

'Your first time for this, is it?' asked Mary-Joy, as she led the way in her slippered feet down a gleaming corridor.

'Uh-huh,' Paula answered.

'So you're a bit nervous, is it?' she said, and this last 'is it?' was sufficient for Paula to place the accent as South African.

Mary-Joy showed Paula into a room that was full of lavender fumes from an oil burner, and had a towel-covered bed in its centre.

'Now take off all your bottom things and just lie down on the bed. Pull up the sheet if you like. I'll be back in a minute and we'll start.'

Paula put her shoes neatly together on the seat of the chair provided, and over the top of them layered her pantyhose, underpants and skirt. Before she left the office, she'd gone into the toilets and wiped herself thoroughly with a KFC refresher towelette, but now she felt nervous all over again about discharges or smears. She plucked a few tissues from a box on a glass shelf and had another go, then tucked the used tissues into the toe of one of her shoes. She hoisted herself up onto the bed and covered her lower half with a thin floral sheet. Mary-Joy was so precisely on time when she returned with a pot of warmed wax and a selection of spatulas, that Paula couldn't help but wonder if there was a peephole in one of the walls.

'Is this going to hurt *really* a lot?' Paula asked. 'Or just a lot?'

'Oh, it's not so comfortable, but it'll be worth it in the end,' Mary-Joy soothed, whisking away the sheet. 'Now, can you tuck your knees up for me? That's it, bend them like that, and can you just hold them there, right against your tummy? I'll be as gentle as I can.'

A Word from Rosie Little
ON PUBIC HAIRSTYLING

Let's consider for a moment the vocabulary that was at the disposal of Paula and Mary-Joy as Paula lay back in a pose she'd not adopted since she was a toddler in the midst of a nappy change. The procedure Paula was about to experience is, of course, most often called the Brazilian. Some of its most famed practitioners are the J Sisters, the Brazilian-born siblings (Janea, Jocely, Jonice, Joyce, Judséia, Juracy, and Jussara) who have really made a name for themselves waxing the living day-lights out of the New Yorkers who visit them in their West 57th Street parlour. In French-speaking countries, however, you might instead request an *epile complet*. And in at least some boutiques, the style is called the Sphinx in honour of a breed of hairless Egyptian cat. Some say that there are actually two styles, the crucial difference being that in the case of the Brazilian a 'landing strip' of hair remains, while the Sphinx leaves nothing at all in its wake.

Just in case you needed proof that up-selling has infiltrated every last nook and cranny of the marketplace, I can tell you that pubic hairstyling does not now end with some kind of soothing ointment being applied to red-raw pudendal skin. You can have your 'landing strip' shaped, curled, spiked or coloured, and you can have applied to your bare skin, in special water-resistant stickers, little *Alice in Wonderland*-inspired messages like FUCK ME. Although you do have to wonder about the intelligence of partners who need a landing strip *and* instructions too.

*

It was not the Brazilian itself, however, that most significantly influenced the events of the night of Paula and Will's anniversary dinner, but the shriek-punctuated conversation that took place between Paula and Mary-Joy at the time it was being performed.

'Special treat for your hubby, is it?' asked Mary-Joy, smoothing on a spatula-load of thick warm wax.

'No, I'm not married yet.'

'Oh, your fiancé then, is it?'

'Ow! Boyfriend, I suppose, is all he is.'

'Oh, that's how it is, is it? Been together long, have you?'

'Two years. Owwww! Shit!'

'Oh, is it? That's quite a while.'

'Are you married?'

'Oh yes,' Mary-Joy said, and Paula could just imagine her being the kind of tiny, dainty little bride who could easily be mistaken for a cake decoration.

'But we were married when we'd known each other for just a few months,' she added.

'Owwwww!'

'You just know, you know? When it's right? You just know. Now just lift your legs a little higher and try to relax your bottom. That's it.'

'You didn't live together first, or anything?'

'Oh no. It's like what my father said when I wanted a car. He could easily have afforded to buy me one, but he said that if I just got what I wanted for free, then I'd never appreciate it.

Now, this little area around the anus here, this can really sting. One, two...'

'Jesus CHRIST!'

There was a small silence.

In which Paula recollected her glimpse of the small, silver cross.

3. Some elementary facts of physics

According to the Ideal Gas Law ($pV=nkT$), the pressure that a gas is under is directly proportional to the number of molecules it contains, provided temperature and volume remain constant. So, since we can safely assume Paula and Will's mouth cavities to be pretty much the same size, and of a roughly equivalent temperature, we need only concern ourselves with how many word-laden oxygen molecules were kicking around in each mouth to find out which set of words was under the most pressure and therefore likely to come spurting out more rapidly. A quick count would have revealed that the number of words it would take Paula, initially at least, to tell Will that it was time he seriously committed to their future together was 163. While Will was only going to need five words (Paula, will you marry me) to make an offer of serious commitment. Which means that the words in Paula's mouth were under 32.6 times more pressure than those in Will's, so there really are no prizes for guessing who got there first.

Paula's voice came out in a taut little squeal.

'I've been doing some thinking, and as you know...obviously…we've known each other for two years now, which is quite some time, and long enough, really, for a job interview. I mean, we've had plenty of time to get to know each other, lived together for a year, quite compatibly I would have thought. Look, perhaps it's my fault. Perhaps I shouldn't have moved in with you, or at least not without clearly setting out some boundaries first. But I was just happy to go with the flow. I thought it would all just happen, naturally. But it hasn't. It hasn't happened. And perhaps it's my fault because I haven't been clear enough about my needs. So I'm going to be very clear, tonight. And just say it. I need to know whether or not this relationship is actually going anywhere, because if it isn't, then we need to make a clean break now, so that I can get on with my life.'

As Will listened to this speech, he felt his balloon deflate by four-fifths of its volume.

'Paula,' he said, for it was the only word he had left in his mouth.

Once it was gone, though, he found that he was high and dry.

Shit, he thought. After all he had done, after all his careful planning, he wanted his proposal of marriage to be just right. Perfect, in fact. He certainly didn't want to arrive at it like this, by way of an ultimatum.

'Honey,' said Will, trying to make his words sound as if they were, indeed, coated in honey. 'Could we talk about something else? It's a special occasion, lovely restaurant. Let's just enjoy it, hey?'

'No, Will. I am setting boundaries. I am being clear. I am letting you know precisely what I want, and all you have to do is provide me with an answer. There are only two possible answers, so it can't be that difficult.'

'Your soup's getting cold. Mmmm. It's very good, actually.'

'I want to have children. I'm sorry, but that's just a fact. You're lucky. You don't have a use-by date, but I do. And if I miss the bus, it's not like there's another one coming along in a minute. What you have to do, Will, is you have to shit, or get off the pot.'

'Honey, can we talk about something else?'

Paula was incredulous. 'No! I want to know. Now. Whether you think this relationship has any future. Or not. I've drawn a line in the sand. And this is it. We've reached it.'

'I respect that. I do. But can we just not have this conversation tonight? Can we not do it right this minute? Could we defer for a day, for an hour even, and just…have a good time?'

'Which is all you ever want to do with me, isn't it?' she said, crossing her legs and wondering if the Brazilian had been a total waste of time, money and excruciating pain. 'You don't want to make a commitment to me, or…marry me. And don't think that it's not hard for me to say that word out loud. What girl wants to have to demand it?'

'Come on, try the soup. It's quite peppery. You'll like it.'

'I do not want to talk about soup, Will. I want to talk about us. And I want to know how it's going to be. Do you want to be with me, permanently, or don't you? That is all I want to know.'

'Not now. Please?'

'Yes. Now. I've decided.'

'Well, I haven't. Please. Just drop it, hey?'

'No. I want to know. Are we going to do the whole thing? Or is this it? Is this the end?'

'Trust me. Please? And drop it?'

'This is not about trust. It's about commitment.'

'You know, you're like a terrier sometimes. See something with fur or feathers and you just will not rest until you've got it between your teeth.'

'I take it that it's over, then?'

'No, no, not at all. Not at all. I did not say that.'

'So you *do* want to marry me?'

'Can we drop this line of questioning?'

'Oh God, how bloody hard is it? Yes, you want to marry me. Or no, you don't.'

'How about at nine o'clock? And we just relax and have a good time until then.'

'What difference is forty-five minutes going to make to you? If you don't know by now, you're not going to get hit by a lightning bolt in the next three-quarters of an hour, are you?'

'Please just drop this.'

'What is it about men that makes them go spastic when a woman — even a woman who lives with them, who cooks their dinners and irons their shirts and scrubs their disgusting skid-marks off the back of the toilet bowl — asks whether or not a relationship is going anywhere?'

'I said "drop it".'

'Don't use that tone with me. I'm not yours to tell what to do. I have things I want to do with my life and I don't want to waste one more minute in a relationship with you if it's not serious. I think that's perfectly fair. Absolutely reasonable.'

'Come on, Paula, shut up.'

'Excuse me?'

'Please shut up. Darling, shut up. Sweetheart, shut up. Trust me, you do not want to have this conversation now.'

'I don't even know why I'm still sitting here, why I'm bashing my head against this brick wall when it's clear that you just don't know how to say it. If you don't want to marry me, then what's the bloody point of us sitting here, all dressed up pretending that there's something to celebrate, when —'

'For fuck's sake!' Will shouted, standing up. 'Here. Look here. See this? It contains an engagement ring. Happy? Are you happy now? Is this how you wanted to get engaged?'

Hush spread through the restaurant in a rapid, unfurling circumference from the epicentre of Paula and Will's table. Other diners fell silent, cutlery suspended, mouths open. They stared at Paula's stunned and silenced face, and at Will, who stood, looking defeated, with a black velvet cube in his fingertips. They watched the cube move away from his fingers, tumbling through the air, a die that landed numberless, with a splash, in Paula's soup.

'I... Will!' she called after him as he threaded his way through tables and chairs to the exit. 'Will! I will!'

But he was already through the glass doors, the thin fabric of his white shirt plastering to his shoulderblades in the breeze. And as the door closed behind him, the hush rolled itself right back up to Paula's feet, allowing her to hear a snicker ricochet from table to table in its wake. There was nowhere for her to look but down at the table, where the splatter-pattern of beef consommé on white linen clearly spelled out just how badly she'd fucked up, and where the mounded shape of the velvet ring-box was resting, like an already-looted treasure chest, in the shallows of her soup.

MARRIAGE

Vision in White

Clocks in international airports do not tell the time. Or not, at least, in the usual way. Gathered together within their auspices are refugees from all quarters of the day: some dazed by the earliness of the morning and others faintly excited to be staying up so late at night. These clocks point their hands at numbers not to signify a particular time of day, but rather to reassure you that the seconds are still being measured, somewhere out there, by the great universal ticktock. The hour is quite arbitrary, and yet I managed to arrive at precisely the wrong time.

It was a huge, gleaming chrome kind of airport, somewhere in Asia. I forget where exactly. The floor was a lake of marble with reflected lights shining just beneath its surface. There were kilometres of duty-free shops and cafés and bars — all closed, because I was in transit during those few hours of local time when the airport shut itself down and went to sleep. I was not alone, of course. There were enough travellers to fill three or four jumbos and we straggled the length of a concourse in a listless and fragmented queue. Those first to arrive had grabbed one of the padded, backless benches that were spaced at intervals down the corridor, while the rest of us sat on the floor or stood leaning against a colossal frosted-glass wall. There was nothing to do. The hours we had to kill would die slow, painful deaths. Surely, I thought, the expression 'terminal boredom' was used for the first time in an airport closed down for the night.

For quite some time, I waited. I did all the things that I imagined would be done by a young woman travelling alone on a holiday she had paid for all by herself, with savings from her first proper job. I creaked open my travel diary to the first, virgin page. And then shut it again. I stared for a while at the type on the pages of the too-literary book that I had been sure would be perfect for the plane.

And then, just for something to do, I went to the Ladies. I sat on the toilet conducting a good close reading of the sanitary napkin advertisement on the back of the door, but remained unconvinced by its wafting, fresh-breeze promises. Still, the advertisement did inspire me to treat myself to the pair of clean knickers in my carry-on bag and to squirt some deodorant around various of my body's moving parts. I had done all that I could think of to do, and so I prepared myself to return to the concourse and resume my boredom. But when I emerged from the cubicle, I saw something I did not expect to see. Standing at one of the marbled basins was a woman in a wedding dress.

'Bugger,' she said, in the way only English women can.

It was not a simple dress. There was sufficient white satin in the skirts and train for Christo to wrap the best part of a one-storey building. There was a mosquito net's worth of tulle tucked into the warp and weft of her hairdo.

'Bugger, bugger, bugger, shit,' said the woman, ferreting in her make-up bag.

'Forgotten something?' I asked.

'Must have left it in the bathroom on the plane. My lipstick. I mean I've got others, but they're all too dark or too bright. It was a really nice peachy colour. Fuck!'

'I've got some pale pink,' I said, holding out a sparkling tube of something called Baby Doll. It had come in one of those gift packs that enable cosmetic firms to offload their most atrocious shades. 'You can have it if you want.'

'Oh, I couldn't.'

'It's all right. I mean I have used it, but I don't have cold sores or anything.'

'That's not what I meant. God. Sorry.'

'Here.'

'Oh, look, could I? This is the closest thing I've got and it's just far too red to wear with white. I'd look like a bloody geisha. I'll only borrow, though.'

'Honestly. Have it. I hardly ever wear lipstick and I suspect your need is greater than mine.'

'It *is* my wedding day,' she said. Then, looking at her watch, 'At least I think it still is.'

She applied the lipstick thickly, and smiled her approval at herself in the mirror.

'Angela,' she said, turning to me and pressing a hand to her heart.

'Rosie.'

And so it was that I met Angela Cuthbert (nee Wootton) and began the conversation — reflected in the mirror of the Ladies' loo — in which I discovered that the reason she had come to be waiting around in her wedding dress in a closed-for-the-night international airport somewhere in Asia was because she had had a vision.

Angela Wootton had seen herself emerging from the silver chrysalis of an aeroplane like a magnificent white butterfly, stepping out onto the staircase and appearing to unfurl as her skirts and veil billowed suddenly in the mild breeze. Against the backdrop of aeroplane and clear sky, she would be a bedizenment of blinding whiteness, the satin of her gown catching the brilliance of the sun. Her new and as-yet-unmet in-laws would watch from the terminal building as she paused at the top of the staircase to wave. And instantly, instantly, they would love her.

It was a vision that came to Angela only gradually, as if from a great distance, moving slowly into the centre of her mind. Once it had settled there, though, she moved it just slightly to one side where she could look upon it whenever she wasn't busy. In quiet moments at work (she was a dental nurse at an inner-city London practice, but wouldn't have to be for too much longer) she would work on the details, deepening the famous blue of the Australian sky and chiselling the handsome features of the flight attendant whose face was just visible over her right shoulder as she turned to wave. For a time, she enjoyed her vision purely as mental celluloid. But on the day that she went to buy her bridal underwear it turned from a vision into a plan.

After a couple of hours and four boutiques, Angela had narrowed the choice to two sets. Each of them had boned corsets in white lace that lashed in her waist and pushed her breasts right up. The difference between them was that while one had suspenders attached and went with high-cut lace knickers, the other finished in a scalloped edge at her hip bones and went with low-cut knickers that made her bum look great, but which would have to be worn with stay-up stockings (not always fabulous for the profile of one's thighs). Now was not the time for a rash decision, Angela counselled herself, remembering her New Year's resolution to take shopping more seriously.

'Look, I'm just too close to the issue to be objective,' she told the shop girl, and went to have a coffee and list the pros and cons of each set on a napkin.

Inside the warm stone walls of the underground café, she toyed with the chocolatey froth of her cappuccino and wished, not for the first time, that Jeremy's mother could see her in all her wedding finery. She had been leaning towards doing the first meeting with Jeremy's parents in lime green three-quarter pants, strappy heels and a white sleeveless polo-neck top. But there in the café, with the turbulent sounds of the coffee machine in the background, a more dramatic idea began to take shape. She nibbled at an almond wafer and wondered if it really were such a silly idea. They were going straight from the reception to the airport anyway. It would be quite dramatic. One of those things you would never forget. She could do it, you know. She would do it. She would wear her gown all the way to Australia. She would step out of the plane, bouquet in hand, as if she had just that minute walked back down the aisle, ready to be sprinkled with confetti and kisses. She would glide across the tarmac to embrace her mother-in-law, who would say, 'You look lovely, dear'. And Angela would smile, and blush just a little.

A Word from Rosie Little
ON BRIDES

It is not, of course, only women already pre-disposed to silliness who can be adversely affected by the distant, promising chimes of wedding bells. If ever a sensible woman is likely to become silly, then it will be in her bride period, which begins, naturally enough, with her engagement and concludes shortly after the wedding, when she emerges from a fog of tulle into the terrible clarity of a world where no-one makes comforting noises for an hour while you sob over the thoughtlessness of a grandmother who refuses to buy any of the gifts specified in the bridal registry; a world in which it suddenly seems conceivable that you might forgive the bridesmaid (bitch!) who got drunk at your hen's night and stole your limelight by bursting messily into tears and declaring that no-one would ever love *her* enough to marry *her*; where the problem of seating Uncle Travis's new young wife (younger than his youngest daughter, you know…) is no longer a valid cause for Camp David-scale diplomacy; a world, in short, suddenly and horribly devoid of the incantation 'whatever you want, darling, it's *your* day'.

I do not think that it is any accident that the croquembouche is a cake traditionally found at nuptial celebrations. I think it the most perfect of metaphors: all those profiteroles piled high on a plate like so many flaky little brides' heads, and within each of them (in place of brains) a quantity of custard: thick and sweet.

*

'Where do your in-laws live?' I asked her as we left the Ladies and returned to the concourse.

'Western Australia. About an hour's flight out of Perth. Loads of Poms there, apparently. And you?'

'Other side. Eastern states, as they say in the West.'

'Oh, really?'

'Why couldn't they make it to the wedding?'

'You won't believe it.'

'I might.'

'Spider.'

'Spider?'

'Jeremy's father was getting his old lawnmower out of the shed. Going to donate it to some trash and treasure thing in the neighbourhood, yeah? Got bitten by a white-tailed spider and had to have his finger amputated. The finger you, you know, give someone the finger with.'

'He couldn't come to your wedding without this particular finger?'

'Well, he was supposed to have knee surgery, you see. And the finger amputation put his knee surgery back and they couldn't afford Business Class and, well, you know what it's like on long flights, even without a dicky knee. So, we said we'd do a little re-enactment when we got there.'

We reached the place on the concourse where Angela and Jeremy had commandeered a pair of facing chaises.

On one of them Jeremy was sleeping, wearing a T-shirt and a pair of shorts. On the other were Angela's bags, which we moved, and an only slightly less than fresh bouquet of orchids and roses, which she placed tenderly in her lap.

'What did Jeremy think?' I asked quietly. 'About you wearing the dress?'

'Oh, he said I was mad.'

'You're mad,' he said.

'But don't you think it would be nice for your mother to actually see me in the gown?'

'Whatever you want, darling, it's *your* day.'

And, indeed, it was her day. It was a tour de force. The pews at the church were decorated with tea roses, the caskets of old violins, and plum-coloured ribbons. The bridesmaids in their voluptuous skirts of raw silk posed like Royal Doulton figurines for the photographer — who had once done a shoot for *Vogue*. At the reception there was the string quartet, and the Viennese waltz was executed faultlessly by the bride and groom, thanks to eight months of dance lessons. And there was the banquet that concluded triumphantly with a towering croquembouche.

The newlyweds took a limo to the airport, and about two hours into the first leg of the journey, Angela cuddled up to her husband across the wide armrests of Business Class and cooed, 'See, it's not so bad, is it?' She had been delightedly fielding the inevitable questions from airline staff and other passengers — 'Yes, we've only been married seven hours', 'Australia', 'No, no, I haven't met them yet'.

She had brought nothing to read on the plane, and didn't want to watch any of the movies since it would involve putting a headset over the top of her hair, thus ruining her do. She had already read the safety instruction card in the seat pocket twice, and thought about the tragedy of being forced to discard her wedding shoes in the event they had to evacuate the aircraft via inflatable slide. The shoes were silk. Like the manicured nail of her ring finger, they were monogrammed with her (new) initials. And they had cost more than she earned in two weeks. After the first meal had been served, a thoughtful flight atten-

dant called Kyle brought her a stack of glossy magazines. She assessed his blond-tipped hair and immaculately filed fingernails. *Probably gay*, she thought. *Shame*.

Angela knew that she should not even glance at the brand new edition of *Bride To Be*. Looking at a bridal magazine hours after you'd tied the knot was just torturing yourself. But look at the magazine she did, and punished she was. Because there in its pages was a wedding ring much nicer than the one that had just a few hours ago been slipped onto the ring finger of her left hand. The magazine ring was beautiful. Stunning. And very original. Rather than the traditional engagement ring and matching wedding ring set — for which Angela had opted — the bride in the magazine had cleverly chosen a single broad band in an opulent arrangement of diamonds and gold. Why hadn't she thought of that?

She had thought that she was really getting somewhere with her impulse buying problem, but here in *Bride To Be* was the proof that she had muffed it on something as important as her wedding jewellery. When, oh when, would she learn that it was *always* worth just popping into the boutique around the corner before you made up your mind?

Still, she reasoned, all was not lost. All she really had to do was put up with her empress-cut diamond engagement ring and plain gold band for a year or two, and then she'd get a new set. She was sure Jeremy wouldn't mind. A fashionable woman couldn't be expected to wear the same jewellery *forever*.

'Are you comfortable in all that?' I asked her.

'Oh, Christ no. My arms are all itchy under the lace and the bones in my corset are jabbing me in the tits.'

She stood up and stretched, rotating her head on her long neck and causing another strand of dark blonde hair to fall from its place in an elaborate construction of loops and love knots. Her interest was caught, for just a moment, by a young man asleep on the marble floor, his girlfriend's dark curls fanning out over his stomach, which she was using for a pillow.

'You can tell *he's* Australian, can't you?' Angela said, sitting down again. 'Look at his legs, they're like trees.'

Jeremy, who had woken by now with ruffled hair, was sitting up reading a finance magazine. His legs, poking out of his navy blue shorts, were thin and darkly haired. He yawned and fiddled just inside one nostril with his finger.

I watched a wave of mild disgust pass over Angela's face before she turned to me.

'Promise me something, Rosie,' she said, in the passionate and sisterly manner that women sometimes affect towards another woman they have chosen as a temporary ally. 'Promise me?'

'What?'

'Promise first.'

'Okay, I promise.'

'Promise me that no matter what you're trying to find, you will always look in the boutique just around the corner before you make up your mind.'

It was not long after I accepted this pearl of wisdom from the bride that her flight was called. As she walked towards the departure gate, trailing a quarter-acre block of white satin, she half-turned back towards me, waving one last goodbye. And I knew, conclusively, that I would never see her again.

And yet her unfinished drama nibbled at the corners of my imagination. Days later, as I strolled by a river in a city full of strange sounds and strange smells, I was still wondering how it had turned out for her. I doubted that she had foreseen she would have to give up her bouquet at customs. I could see her, batting her eyelids at the chaps in uniform, asking what on earth the signs about rotting fruit and sticky little fruit flies had to do with her lovely flowers? The customs guys would have been unmoved, I imagined, but would, out of kindness, have waited until Angela had crossed through the big, swinging doors before they tossed the white roses and pink orchids into a grubby airport bin.

'Why didn't you tell me?' she would ask Jeremy.

'Never mind, baby, we'll get you a fresh bunch.'

'But it won't be the same.'

'It doesn't matter, babe.'

'It matters to me! But clearly, you don't care about that!'

Yes, she would snap like that, and then immediately wish that she hadn't. She would know that brides did not snap. Brides were poised, calm, happy.

Pull yourself together, Angela! she would tell herself. *This is your honeymoon.*

It was a word that had tasted so sweet in the Piccadilly travel agency. *Hon-ey-moon.* She had felt its syllables melt in her mouth as she dished it out to the mousy girl behind the counter, who no doubt wished that she were going to Australia on her honeymoon. Yes, thought Angela, she was in an enviable position, orchids or no orchids. And so she edited the bouquet from her vision and accentuated instead the princess-style wave.

As the Cuthberts settled into their domestic airline seats for the final leg of the journey, Angela took her husband's hand. She smiled like a film star as she saw a touch of light spark off the gold band on her finger. Only an hour more. One single hour, a little circle of time the same size as the face of her Raymond Weil watch (which, of course, perfectly matched Jeremy's). Once the seatbelt sign was switched off, a stewardess in a taut navy suit presented the newlyweds with a small bottle of champagne and two plastic goblets.

'We would like to help you celebrate your special day,' she said in broad Australian, smiling.

It was a windy, bushfire kind of a day and the flight was bumpy. Unbalanced by a pocket of turbulence, the stewardess pitched into Angela's white satin lap the full glass of red wine that was destined for the gentleman in the next row. Very, very deep down, Angela knew that it wasn't the girl's fault. But the knowledge was too deep to prevent her from shrieking, 'You stupid cow! Look at my dress! Do you have any idea, any faint conception, how much this dress cost? No! Of course you don't! And you've just wrecked it, you stupid, careless...slut!'

The stewardess began fervently to apologise and mop at the spilled wine.

'Don't touch! Don't touch it! Just don't make it any worse

than it already is, you ridiculous, brainless trolley dolly.'

'Look, I'm sorry, she doesn't mean it. It's been a really long day,' Jeremy intervened.

'How dare you? How dare you take her side?'

'Well, you are being a bit irrational.'

And Angela saw, twiddling with the corners of her husband's mouth, a tiny little smile.

'Are you laughing at me?'

'Well, you do…I'm sorry, love. You do look a bit funny.'

And Angela flounced out of her seat and down the aisle to the tiny toilet cubicle, which she almost entirely filled with her froth of wine-stained skirts, and began to cry. When her tears subsided, she looked at herself in the mirror. Under the harsh cast of the fluorescent lights she was all blotchy and creased. Somewhere in their travels, they must have crossed some kind of dateline. Which meant it was all over. It was no longer her day.

She was not so easily defeated, though. She wiped the mascara from beneath her eyes and breathed in deeply, a sense of determination filling her lungs. She returned to her seat and sat beside Jeremy in a restrained silence (not, you understand, a sulk) until the plane landed and taxied to a standstill.

'Congratulations on your marriage. And I'm really sorry,' said the clumsy stewardess, passing down Angela's bags from the overhead locker.

'I'm sure you didn't mean it,' Angela said. There was no sense holding a grudge on one's wedding day. Brides were supposed to be happy. And gracious. And since no-one else, clearly, was going to make an effort to make her happy, then she would just have to be bigger than all of them and do it herself.

At the door of the plane, she prepared herself. She would step out, smile, and wave. Step out. Smile. Wave. But when she stepped out, it was into the ferocious cross-current of a dusty wind that tore the tulle from her hair and carried it away over the tarmac into the neighbouring pine plantation.

It was an extraordinary mime that Mr and Mrs Cuthbert Senior witnessed from behind the glass of Arrivals. In the blustery conditions, Angela's wine-dappled skirts were a handicap, billowing out to one side as she struggled down the first few steps. It's unlikely that silk wedding pumps, even those that cost more than two weeks' salary, are ever designed with grip in mind. Which is why Angela, about halfway down the stairs, slipped and fell on her bottom, upon which she slid the rest of the way to the ground.

'Ouch! Poor lass!' Jeremy's mother said, muffling a giggle with her handkerchief.

As in a good silent movie, captions were largely superfluous to the interpretation of the scene that followed. The Cuthberts could see that although Jeremy rushed to rescue his damsel, he was having trouble stopping himself from laughing. They could see, too, that from Angela's point of view, her mishap was entirely Jeremy's fault. Her lips were forming all kinds of words that the seasoned watcher of test cricket telecasts could easily decipher. Jeremy submitted to the tirade for a time, then threw his arms in the air and turned to march towards the terminal building.

'Not bad for a first domestic,' said Mr Cuthbert Senior as Angela hurled one monogrammed silk pump, then the other, at Jeremy's head.

Jeremy threw one of the shoes back over his shoulder, in the general direction of Angela, but his high lob pass was intercepted by the ruck rover from the Sharks, the local Aussie Rules footie team on its way back from an end-of-season drinking marathon. It was a good mark, and his team-mates cheered and called for the handball. Angela chased after one of them, which only had the effect of egging the lads on in a game of keepings-off. A rogue gust blew her skirts up around her face, giving the footballers a good view of a set of high-cut knickers and suspenders.

That's where I left her: whirling in perpetuity, piggy white-frock in the middle, chasing after a monogrammed shoe.

I admit that I am a coward and that I left her there because I could not bear to watch the next scene. I could bring her within metres of her in-laws, but no closer. I had reached a point in the story equivalent to the moment in a radio station prank call when I would always switch channels, or the moment in the movie when the joke-butt hero embarrassed himself one time too many, causing me to squirm right out of my seat and leave the cinema in the dark. And yet it is odd, isn't it? That I should get squeamish, when I was the one who pushed her down the stairs in the first place.

Slightly guilty, faintly remorseful, I returned to the point in the story where Angela stood at the top of the staircase, and stood there with her for a time, right there at the locus of her spectacular vision. And I thought that perhaps I should not have caused her to slip. Perhaps I should have had more compassion. Perhaps her silliness did not deserve quite so humiliating a punishment. But the longer I paused there, the clearer it became to me that her tumble down the staircase was, in fact, beyond my control. I realised that it was inevitable — written in the proverbs, even — that Angela Cuthbert (nee Wootton) would end up on her arse. For I doubted that anyone had ever more perfectly embodied the quintessence of bride before a fall.

WORK

Rosie Little's Brilliant Career

Once upon a time (and I use these words advisedly, in the fervent hope that the sisterhood has by now worked its magic, and things have changed) the demographics of the average newspaper office were enough to make a girl despair. While the vast majority of the reporters were bright and ambitious young women (for ambitious, read 'desperate to get into television'), most of the subeditors were middle-aged blokes. Divorced, alcoholic blokes, I might add, through whose embittered kidneys the reporters' prose was destined to pass. The rest of the subs were mothers: former twenty-something reporters who'd come back part time after their maternity leave, bringing with them leftovers in Tupperware containers and repertoires of alarming anecdotes about pelvic floor muscles and mastitis. And, of course, all those who made crucial decisions behind the frosted glass of private offices were men roughly the same age as my grandfather.

Especially during the long, slow hours of nightshift, when I sat at the night reporter's desk, edgy from too much caffeine and not enough food, I was prone to casting my eye around the office and wondering what was my destiny? It couldn't be television: I didn't have smooth hair. Did that mean I would have to get myself a nice wardrobe of pastel suits and bail out into PR? Or would that be me, sitting over there at the subs table wearing a tartan shirt with a Peter Pan collar, eating my microwaved dinner and telling people who weren't listening how many stitches I'd had after my last episiotomy? Please no, I begged anyone in the cosmos who would listen, please don't let that be me. But please, don't let me be Lorna, either.

Lorna was that anomalous creature, a woman who had survived in a newsroom to middle age and attained a position of seniority to boot. So long had she been sitting in the chief sub's chair, shoulders rolled forward and chin stuck out, that her body had begun to look as if it were sitting down even when, technically speaking, it was standing up. Either way, the fleshy fold of her lower stomach lay over the top of her thighs like a thick apron, then her upper stomach folded down, in turn, over the lower stomach, followed by the uppermost layer of a heavy and apparently unsupported bosom.

Lorna was a very still person. She was quite still even when she was typing fast, and the way her fingers flicked and kicked on the end of motionless wrists put me in mind of an Irish dancer's legs. Her stillness was not benign, however. She used it in much the same way as a crocodile does: lying there inert, lulling her intended prey into thinking it's standing beside nothing more dangerous than a log of petrified wood. But, in fact, a crocodile can move as fast as a racehorse over a short distance, and when it does, you can easily find yourself with your jugular vein dangling down around your sternum. To the left-hand side of the chief sub's chair, it was possible to discern a slight deviation in the walking track that had been worn into the carpet, and it only took new copy boys a day or two to discover why it was advisable to follow it.

'Incompetence. Nothing I hate more than incompetence,' Lorna would mutter, settling back into reptilian stillness while some fresh-faced graduate bled quietly from multiple cuts inflicted by the sharp edge of her tongue.

Or else she'd repeat, through barely opened lips: 'Six months. Six more months. Six months and I'm out of here.'

It was a well-known fact that Lorna was leaving in six months' time, since Lorna had been leaving in six months' time for close to twenty-five years. It was even said that when she first accepted the job — back in the days when the newsroom rang with the cheerful TING! of typewriter return carriages and reporters were allowed to chain-smoke at their desks — Lorna shook the editor's hand and said she was only staying for six months. But I never did believe that story, for the simple reason that it failed to account for Oscar. Bringing a pot plant to the office, I believe, is a sign of quite serious commitment.

The sum total of the affection that I could muster for Lorna was contingent on the image that I had of her arriving for work on her very first day, with Oscar. I dressed her for the occasion in a taupe-coloured skirt and jacket, and recoloured her long, greying hair in an appealing shade of light brown. I gave her glasses, and while it is true that they were heavy-rimmed and unflattering, the overall effect of them was to suggest that this plain and sturdy-limbed young woman might harbour any number of intriguing mysteries. And this intimation of suppressed sentiment was only strengthened by the presence of the young *monstera* — nothing more than a single tender stem and a pair of leaves resembling a child's outstretched hands — growing, greenly, in the earthenware pot Lorna held in the crook of her arm.

Over the course of the ensuing years, Oscar grew into and out of a succession of pots. An especially big move came when he was forced, by a combination of his own virulent growth and the advent of the new computer terminals, off the desktop and onto the floor beside Lorna's feet. By the time my own first day in the newsroom arrived, Oscar was housed in a colossal black plastic tub to the right-hand side of the chief sub's chair. He was more of a tree than a pot plant by now, and his trunk had thickened to match the diameter of Lorna's ankle.

I remember my first Monday at the paper as a hopeful day for both of us. I arrived early in order to settle in, and while I pinned my favourite photographs and quotations to the felted surface of my cubicle divider, and set out on my desk a small, framed painting of an apple by my now-quite-famous–artist friend Eve, Oscar reached out and brushed — for the very first time, with the tip of his uppermost leaf — the pale ceiling panel of electrical light that he had mistaken for the sun.

If we were to leap ahead by four years, however, we would find that same leaf pointing dejectedly down to the ground. Oscar's trunk had, during that time, reached the ceiling and performed a U-turn, and now a strong, green curve of it was braced against the disappointment of the lighting panel.

And as for me?

Well, I had come to understand how it might feel to be the daughter of a boastful miller. I'm sure you remember the tale: the one in which a miller (in order to make himself appear a person of great importance) tells a king that he has a daughter who can spin straw into gold. The king puts the miller's daughter into a room with a spinning wheel and a pile of straw, which she must turn into gold by morning, if she values her life.

'Here's a handful of hearsay,' the editor would say to me before retreating behind his pane of frosted glass.

'Spin me forty centimetres of copy by nightfall, there's a good girl.'

'Here's half a rumour and a skerrick of unsubstantiated fact,' he would say the next day. 'Sixty centimetres by nightfall, if you value your life.'

And sometimes what was required of me was to spin column centimetres out of nothing at all.

'So, what do you like best about maths?' I would crouch down to ask Bruno, the seven-year-old winner of a nationwide Grade Four mathematics tournament, while he made dripping-water sounds with his tongue inside his cheek.

'Dunno.'

'What do you think you'd like to be when you grow up?'

'Dunno.'

'How do you feel about winning the competition?'

'Dunno.'

'How will you spend the prize money, do you think?'

'Dunno.'

Are you actually retarded, or just a little shit? No, no, please, don't tell me, I think I can guess...

Or I would ask: 'What's the secret of your longevity, Mr Grosvenor?' — shouting in order to be heard by the one hundred-year-old man who had lost all his inhibitions along with his bladder control and nine-tenths of his vision.

'Nice tits,' he'd say, as drool dripping from the tip of his chin fizzled out one of the candles on his birthday cake.

'Oh, I'm so sorry,' his embarrassed and almost equally aged daughter would say, catching his hand before it dipped down the neck of my shirt. 'My father was always such a gentleman.'

By way of some rudimentary alchemy I usually managed to produce sufficient words to accompany the pictures. ('Ask seven-year-old maths whiz Bruno Crawford for the secret of his success and he'll tell you it's repetition.'/'Terry Grosvenor may be one hundred years old, but his appreciation of life's pleasures remains undimmed.') The trouble was, the alchemy did not cease when I filed my copy and went home to bed. My nights were sometimes sleepless for wondering what further transformation was being wrought upon a story that would bear my by-line.

'Please,' said a senior Health Department bureaucrat, the latest Rumplestiltskin to whom I had promised my firstborn child if only he would help me spin this day's quotient of straw into column centimetres. 'Please remember that I'm only doing this interview on the understanding that you don't use the word "epidemic". We are not talking about an epidemic here, just a few isolated cases of glandular fever, and we don't want people unduly alarmed.'

'Oh please, no,' I said the next morning when I walked to the corner shop to get some milk, and was confronted by the day-bills for our newspaper screaming teen kissing bug epidemic shock from within their metal cages.

A Word from Rosie Little
ON NEWSPAPER HEADLINES

It's said that sport is the civilised society's substitute for war, and also that the games we play as children are designed to prepare us for the realities of adult life. Certainly it's true that my brother thrived in the capitalist kindergarten of the Monopoly board, developing a set of ruthless strategies whose success is reflected in his bank balance even to this day. I, on the other hand, can still be undone by the kind of ridiculous sentimentality that would see me sacrifice anything, *anything*, in order to have the three matching red-headed cards of Fleet Street, Trafalgar Square and The Strand sitting tidily together on my side of the board.

Working late shifts in a newsroom allows for plenty of time to ruminate on how childhood board game strategy might act as an early indicator of career success, and even to come up with the basics of a board game to prepare aspiring journalists for the life in the fourth estate. I call it HEADLINE DEADLINE.

A game for four players, HEADLINE DEADLINE closely approximates the actual process by which newspaper headlines are chosen on a daily basis. I won't bore you with the intricate details of the game; suffice to say that the set comes with two decks of cards, one of which is made up of cards bearing a single word (SHOCK, TERROR, PLUNGE, EPIDEMIC, PLEA, THREAT, TRAGIC, ETC.), while the other is made up of cards bearing newsworthy scenarios, for example:

An elderly woman was hospitalised yesterday and treated for shock after a youth burst into a hairdressing salon with a water pistol. The youth, who is understood to be unhappy with a haircut he received at the same establishment the previous day, squirted the hairdresser with the high-power toy gun, warning her that he was not her only unhappy customer.

The players must use their stock of single-word cards to come up with a headline to fit the scenario before a ninety-second time limit expires. For the above scenario we might get SIEGE SHOCK TERROR, for example. Or TRAGIC TEEN GUNMAN HORROR. Or VIOLENCE EPIDEMIC THREAT, perhaps.

It is possible that the prototype set of headline deadline, which was slapped together with materials from the art department during a succession of slow news nights, still lurks dustily beneath my old desk. But it is unlikely that anyone will ever create a more perfect headline than the one devised in just seventy-six seconds on a Monday night when there was no news at all (due to the malfunction of the newsroom's fax machine):

NAKED HELICOPTER

NUN'S PLEA

The brilliance of this headline has eclipsed my memory of the scenario that spawned it, but I'm sure it doesn't matter. Sales would have soared.

*

It was nightshift on the Christmas Eve that marked my four years and one month's service at the paper, and by way of a concession to the festive season I had worn to the office my six-teen-hole cherry-red Doc Martens. I was on the phone to a policeman who could reasonably expect to spend his Christmas Eve answering the phone every hour, on the hour, to me and my cheery voice asking, 'Anything happening?'

'No, not a sausage,' he said, as patiently as he could manage.

I put down the phone and called the fire brigade, the ambulance service and the talking clock, only because it didn't sigh at me as if to say 'not you again'.

'If I saved really hard,' I reasoned with myself after I'd said a fond farewell to the talking clock, 'I could be out of here in six months.'

The phrase echoed in my mind and tripped the alarm on an early-warning system. *Out of here in six months*. Had I really just thought that? My heart stopped for a pico-second and my eyes shot to the chief sub's chair. Which was empty.

'Where's Lorna?' I called out over the din of the subs' table. Surely the magic pudding of her six more months had not finally run out? The night subs had already sunk a couple of cartons and in their red and white Santa hats they resembled a pack of aged and feral elves.

'Don't panic, she's only having a couple of weeks off,' said one of the elves, leaning back in his chair and scratching his scrotum. 'Oh, fuck! I'm supposed to water Oscar.'

Oscar, doubling as the office Christmas tree, was drizzled with red and gold tinsel. An angel had been hanged by the neck from one his highest branches.

'I promised I wouldn't let you down, Lorna baby!' the sub shouted as he directed a stream of pungent yellow piss into the pine bark at the base of Oscar's trunk.

'Anything happening?' I asked the on-duty policeman, brightly, an hour later.

'No, not a sausage,' he said wearily.

'Anything happening?' I asked the on-duty firefighter.

'Nothing,' he said firmly.

'Anything happening?' I asked the on-duty ambulance officer.

'Honestly, you people. Can't you take a rest? It's Christmas Eve,' he whined.

'How are you, darling?' I asked the talking clock.

'At the third tone, it will be seven-oh-six and twenty seconds,' he replied.

'You sound a little lacklustre,' I said. 'Everything all right?'

'At the third tone it will be seven-oh-six and thirty seconds,' he said, and I knew just how he felt.

'Anything happening?' I asked the on-duty policeman, another hour later.

'No, not a sausage,' he said even more wearily.

'Come on, it's Christmas. There must be something. Anything.'

'Well…'

'Yes?'

'It's just a whisper at this stage. Don't know much about it myself.'

'Hmmm?'

'We've just sent our divers down to the waterfront. Some poor bastard's bobbed up near one of the docks.'

We didn't cover suicides; apparently it encouraged them. But if it was anything else — accident, mystery, murder — it was a story.

'You're a legend,' I said after he gave me the precise location.

I took a car to the scene, but parked it and its newspaper numberplates several blocks back from the water. Once out of the car, I concealed my notebook and pen by shoving them down the back of my skirt, beneath the hem of my cardigan. I was experienced enough to know that regular, just-passing-by nosiness was regarded by the authorities as much less abhorrent than the professional kind in which I specialised.

As I strolled down to the docks, I let my imagination out on a short leash. What would this corpse look like? Would it be bloated and blue? Would its extremities have been nibbled by crustaceans, or its eyes sucked out by eels? Would it be some-body I knew? A face I recognised? I entertained several deli-ciously morbid scenarios, but was forced to dismiss them just as soon as I saw that the divers had already done their work. One of them, his dripping wetsuit making a puddle on a concrete walkway, was zipping up a body bag, while the other was standing by the back of his utility, towel-drying the bare top half of his body. An ambulance was manoeuvring in the car park, readying itself for a swift pick-up.

I slunk around the side of the utility, pausing to observe a plastic bag full of toys, still encased in their retail packaging, lying on the passenger seat alongside a roll of gaudy Christmas wrapping paper. I pictured the following morning's scene in the diver's home: his little dressing-gowned poppets, half-crazed on some kind of sugar-coated breakfast cereal, tearing that awful paper off their presents with squeals of glee.

'Hello,' I said, presenting my hand to the diver, who was buttoning up a warm-looking shirt.

'Hello.'

'I'm Rosie Little. I'm a reporter,' I apologised.

'Well, at ease, Ms Little. We've been expecting him. Chucked himself in a couple of days ago. So it's nothing for you to worry about.'

'You're sure?'

'Quite.'

'Thanks,' I said. 'And Merry Christmas.'

'You're working late,' he said, in a prolongation of the conversation that was most unexpected.

'Until midnight,' I replied, cautiously delighted.

'And what happens then?'

He wrapped a towel around his waist and from beneath it tugged off his wetsuit while I did my best not to watch.

'Depends which story I'm in, I suppose.'

'Don't you know?'

'No, not anymore.'

'Well, I hope it's not the one with the pumpkin.'

'No, no. Definitely not that one.'

'Got time for a quick Christmas drink, then?' he asked, pulling on a pair of jeans and nodding towards the nearby pub, its outside tables packed with drinkers on the verge of a holiday.

He introduced himself as Paddy and bought two beers, and while we drank them we talked about diving for pleasure rather than for dead bodies. I was charmed by the small specks of sea salt that had crystallised in his dark eyelashes and eyebrows.

'You know,' I said, 'I rather had the impression that you had someone to go home to.'

'Oh?'

'The Barbie doll and the cricket set in the front of your ute.'

'Oh?'

'Trained observer, you see.'

'Well, Rosie Little, trained observer, you didn't stop to think perhaps that I might have nieces and nephews?'

'An uncle? Who doesn't outsource his present-buying? What's wrong with your mother?'

'She's dead.'

'Oh God, I'm sorry.'

'Forget it. No, really, forget it. Have another drink, and tell me…Do you always go to work in outlandish red boots?'

'I would love to tell you, but I'd better be getting back to the office,' I said, allowing him a full view of my reluctance.

'I'd like to see you again,' he said, and I responded with something part way between a shy smile and a smirk.

He handed me a card inscribed with his full name: PATRICK WOLFE. Which transformed my smile into one of the regretful kind in which the corners of your mouth turn down rather than up.

'I'm sorry,' I said, as much to myself as to him, for I had been beginning to like him quite a bit.

'Why? Do *you* have someone to go home to?'

'No. It's all to do with nominative determinism I'm afraid, Mr Wolfe,' I said, still smiling.

He polished off his beer and upended the froth-lined pot on the bar towel.

'Grrr,' he said, and I was pleased to see that his face wore a regretful smile of its own.

I slunk back into the office by the side door and slithered in behind the night reporter's desk. But to no avail. The nerviest of the paper's photographers was pacing, anxiously, in his too-white sneakers and multi-pocketed vest.

'The fuck have you been?' he asked. Not waiting for an answer, he said, 'You'd better come and have a look at these.'

On a large computer screen, he clicked through a raft of photographs of a suburban house reduced to charcoal. My pulse picked up speed. Where was this? When was this? They were good shots, some of yellow-clad firemen amid smoke and flames, but mostly of shocked family members staring at the charred and dripping-wet framework of a ruined home.

'When was this?' I asked.

'About quarter past eight. I couldn't find you, so I just went.'

'I've been checking the rounds all night. The bloody fire

brigade told me there was nothing on.'

'Look at *this*, though. *This* is the shot. *This* is the front page,' he said, and I had to agree.

It was a wide-angle shot of the scene, and in the foreground was a small golden-haired girl in a polka-dot dress, one angelic cheek lightly touched with soot. In her arms she held the blackened remains of a Christmas wreath that had been hanging on the now-unhinged front door. Her lower eyelids were brimming with tears. Nauseating. Perfect.

'And I missed it,' I said mournfully.

'Yup.'

'Did you get any words?'

'I got the kid's name. Madison Jones. She's four and a half.'

'And that's it? That's all you know?'

'Yup.'

'I'm in Deep Shit.'

'Yup.'

'Or not,' I said. 'Just the one "d" in Madison?'

'Yup. Why? What are you going to do?'

'The same thing I do every day,' I said grimly.

And at my desk, I began to spin.

An hour and a half later the first edition of the Christmas Day paper rolled off the press and into the hands of the editor. He called me into his office, and as his high-backed chair swung around, he came to face me with an inscrutable look that induced a sharp pang of conscience.

'Gold,' he said, his face breaking into a smile. 'Absolute gold.'

He gestured to the copy of the paper lying on his desk, its front page almost entirely filled with the image of little flaxen-haired Madison before the wreckage of her family home. Beneath her, in six-trillion point Bodoni, was a quote lifted from my story, which appeared in full on page three. It read: 'But what if Santa doesn't know where to find me?'

'Fancy her saying that, hey?' the editor said, shaking a grandfatherly head, and I saw for the first time how pure was his willingness to believe that I truly could spin straw into just his kind of gold.

'Fancy,' I replied softly.

'Magic,' the editor said, plonking down on the desk in front of me a bottle of champagne. 'Looks like it's about time we started to expect a bit more of you, doesn't it?'

It was in order to postpone the vision of my daily pile of straw growing to mountainous dimensions that, once I left his office, I popped the champagne cork, downed one cupful, poured myself another and joined the subs in their raucous and tuneless carolling. 'I saw Mummy blowing Santa Claus, under-neath the mistletoe last night,' we sang, until the tower clock next door chimed in another Christmas Day.

Nightshift over, the office was strewn with plastic cups, vanquished bottles, emptied bags of potato chips, early copies of the first edition and the odd drunken, sleeping subeditor: so much rubbish for the cleaners to deal with in due course. I flopped into Lorna's chair and lay my head on the paper-thin pillow of a day-bill that declared CHRISTMAS BLAZE TRAGEDY SHOCK. Through the floor I could feel the vibrations of the press, still churning deep in the bowels of the building, still replicating my golden little lies.

In that shallow, woozy sleep, I dreamed that Oscar, with one flex of his serpentine trunk, dislodged the plastic covering of the lighting panel that had teased him for so long. Then, with his upper trunk, he forced the housing of the light fixture up and into the ceiling cavity, revealing a tangle of red and black wiring, as well as the silver lining of the roof itself. He slid one leaf into the overlap between two sheets of insulation, and began to thump with a coiled green fist on the underside of the roofing tiles. Soon, the silver sheeting split wide open, and clumps of terracotta showered the office floor, allowing a refreshing draught of night-cooled air to pour in. Through the hole in the roof could be seen a segment of dark sky, the stars like gleaming sword-points upon which veils of wispy cloud were tearing themselves to shreds. In place of the moon was the illuminated rim of the clock face on the tower next door.

Then someone else stepped into my dream, and up onto the rim of Oscar's tub. She grasped the plant's trunk in two hands and there was a slight creaking sound as she placed one foot on the lowest of his branches. Steadily, she began to climb, hand over hand, up through the leaves, around and around as if Oscar's branches were the steps of a helix-like ladder. She came into view, and went out again, obscured now and then by foliage. In some glimpses, she wore a taupe-coloured suit, thick pantyhose and unflattering heavy-rimmed glasses, and in others, she was a small child with golden curls and a polka-dot dress. Up and up she went, up towards the open, beckoning sky. And when I woke, I knew that it was time for me to follow.

LONGING

Lonely Heart Club

JULIA

Although she had recently attained the age of thirty-five, Julia was determined that she would not panic. No, she would not panic. She would simply continue to water the tomatoes. They were in pots on her balcony, tangling their furry stems around the balustrade. She would continue to coax out their heavy green baubles, and try to keep these to their promises of redness. She would continue, too, to take her vitamin tablets each morning and to drink six glasses of water a day, to have her legs waxed and her hair cut every six weeks. She would continue sweltering in Bikram yoga class on Monday nights, trying to master the half-tortoise, and come to terms with farting in public, which her instructor said was important. She did not want him to think that she was anal — a danger she would know to have been averted when she no longer felt the impulse to clench her buttocks in order to keep the volume down.

And she would continue going to work, although this was

no trouble at all. At the leather and pipe-smoke legal practice, she was one of the cleverest in a clever bunch, but less likely than any of the others to accessorise her cleverness with displays of ego. She conducted herself calmly (although she would never acquiesce) and even the senior partners sought her counsel. At work she was *only* thirty-five, and there was certainly no need to panic.

At thirty-five, Julia was well and truly old enough to know that nothing good came from panic, or haste, or recklessness. You could not even buy a good pair of shoes with them. To begin, now, to frequent bars or take tennis lessons would be only to guarantee disappointment. She had observed thirty-five-year-old friends doing precisely these things, and had served well-intended dinners to the human oddments with whom they were now trying to make a life. No. She had drawn the hopscotch squares of her pavement, and she would not put a foot beyond them, even if she was thirty-five. And so in her continuing way she went, on Saturday mornings, to sit in the warm café on her generally cold street. There, she continued to drink mocha that she continued to prefer weighted towards the chocolate rather than the coffee. And she read. Newspapers, or books of serious literary intent, while her hand-knitted scarf purred over the back of her chair.

ERIN

It was too late now. And yet, only a fraction of a second before it had happened, it had been too early. Too early. Too late. Nothing in between. Not even the smallest of windows that she might have picked if she had been especially alert. The edges of too early and too late had fused together and Erin had known herself to be once again excluded; sealed forever beyond and outside the world in which Bella moved with all the bright, swaying confidence of a flame atop a candle.

What had happened was that Bella had given Erin a rock. Bella had been barefoot and up to her knees in the topaz-coloured water of a mountainside lake, grimacing and giggling at the sensation of icy water on feet hot and blistered from three days of boots and constant walking. She had looked down between her pale, suppurating toes and seen something. With one hand capturing her long curly hair in a makeshift ponytail, she had bent down and reached into the lake. Then, yelping and holding her prize high in the air, she had run, splashing through the shallow water, to the shore where Erin lay on the pebbled beach.

Into Erin's hand she had pressed a small and improbable rock, dark red in colour and in the precise shape of a heart. Not a human heart, blobby and irregular, but a Valentine's heart of perfect symmetry; the kind of shape that might be stitched in scarlet satin, or cut out of shiny paper.

'A heart for a dear heart,' Bella said, as she gave Erin the rock. Then, flopping down on the pebbles and laying her grinning head in Erin's lap, she said: 'I do love you, you know.'

She said it like someone who had so much love to sprinkle around that she could afford to be careless with it, like someone dusting a cake with icing sugar and letting drifts of it fall onto the floor. It was a gesture that Erin ought to have been able to accept in the blithe and utterly Bella-like spirit in which it was given, but it only made her feel more a floor and less a cake. And she knew, the second the sweet, meaningless dust of those words settled over her, that it was too late. She thought of, and regretted, all those times — over coffee, tea, or cold creek water — that she had encouraged Bella to keep talking, confiding, about boyfriends past and present, and allowed the sound of Bella's voice to prevent her own silence from being heard. She felt for the weight of the stone in her hand and it was both heavy and light at once. It meant just too much, and not nearly enough. There was no way that she could tell her now.

On the final day of the trek, Erin walked behind Bella, no longer smiling at the amusing way she paddled with her hands through the air at her sides, but planning out the steps of their friendship's attrition. They would graduate in just a few weeks in any case, and it was commonplace, surely, for university friends to simply go their separate ways.

In the horizontal light of the early evening, they emerged from the bush to find Derek and his car waiting to collect them. Bella let the weight of her pack fall to the ground and flew towards him, arms outstretched like the wings of a plane.

'Do I stink?' she asked, raising her arms high. 'Do I pong? Do I really, really reek?'

He sniffed one of her armpits deeply and crossed his eyes before pulling her close, one hand travelling, habitually it seemed to Erin, down to squeeze her backside.

Erin had no doubt that Derek loved Bella. But it was likely that he loved her for all the obvious reasons and not for the way she always nursed her teacup tenderly in two hands, as if she were scared she might crush its delicate painted blooms. Not for the way she signed off her emails with the nom de plume Tintinnabula, or for the fact that she could fold six different animals in sticky-note origami. Not because she could sing 'Twinkle Twinkle Little Star' in Latin, or because she was childishly afraid of thunderstorms. It was likely that he loved her because she was lovely, and not because she was perfect.

A Very Quick Word from Rosie Little

Mica, mica, parva stella
Miror quaenam sis tam bella
Super terra parva pendes
Alba velut gemma splendes
Mica, mica, parva stella
Miror quaenam sis tam bella
(just in case you were wondering…)

*

JULIA

On a night when Julia was alone on her couch and had continued to watch television well beyond the point at which her interest had expired, she saw a science program about falling in love. On the screen, faceless young bodies in blue denim writhed in a crowded nightclub while a plummy English voice spoke, rather too excitedly, of physiological cause and effect, of hormones and synapses. As if she needed reminding. As if she needed anyone rubbing it in that there was a prosaic explanation for everything. Now even the mysteries of attraction could be reduced to the cellular level, to the manipulative strategising of ambitious DNA. She punched the off button on the remote control and sat for a moment with the lingering echo of the television's high-pitched drone in her ears.

ERIN

Erin graduated and moved to a new and larger city. She began what she hoped would be a long and distinguished diplomatic career in a bottom-rung job that still paid well enough for her to afford the rent on a beautiful apartment and a small fraction of its jacaranda umbrella-ed garden.

A new life spread out before her like a bolt of beautiful green cloth, and she knew that she held the scissors in her own hand. But into this new life she had brought a stowaway.

Erin could not bring herself to throw the rock away, but neither did she want to confirm its significance by deliberately giving it a place. To set it on the shelf of one of her apartment's art deco nooks, or even to tuck it away inside a jewellery box with her prefect's badge, would be to name it as something to be treasured, remembered or regretted. So she compromised by putting it in the bottom drawer of the bathroom cabinet with a packet of cotton balls, some after-sun moisturiser and an exquisite but ultimately useless cloisonné manicure set which had caught her eye at a trash and treasure stall and had never been opened since. But a few months later she rediscovered the rock in the heat of a sunburn, and so she relocated it to the bottom of the peg basket, where it stayed until a thunderstorm blew the basket off the line and scattered bright plastic pegs all over the lawn and left only the little heart resting in the plastic weave of the basket as if caught in a net. And so it went, this solo game of hide-and-not-seek, until one of Erin's workmates — a sparkly, newly married woman called Nikki, who had different-coloured hair each week and a pinprick stud above the flare of one nostril — invited her home for dinner.

Nikki and her husband were in love. They flitted around each other like a pair of gorgeous rainforest birds, performing well-rehearsed stories of courtship and travel, finishing each other's sentences on precisely the right notes. Erin was, for a time, too absorbed in her hosts' antics and in the gleaming, primary brightness of the many blown-glass artefacts in their ultra-modern home to notice that the dinner table was set for four. It was a fact that she registered only when the doorbell rang and Nikki jumped up from the table to answer it, irrepressible excitement showing on her face.

His name was Tom. And he was good-looking and clever and charming. He was well dressed and well informed, with faultless politics and neat brown hands that roundly shaped the air as he emphasised soundly made points. Over dinner, he and Erin talked book and film, and discovered a mutual dislike of right-wing newspaper columnists and shared passions for cooking and rock-climbing. So engaged was Erin in conversation with him that she was even able to ignore Nikki and her husband winking at each other over the top of electric-blue wineglasses.

'Maybe we could, you know, catch up for a drink sometime,' Tom said after dinner, when their hosts were in the kitchen, carolling to each other as they cleared away dishes. Erin had just plucked off the back of her chair the winter-weight coat that she had brought with her in case she felt like walking home on this late-autumn night.

'You know, a drink?' he prompted, smiling and miming the elbow bend.

One of these days, she would work out what to say in these situations. One of these days, she would be ready. Prepared. A response that was at once witty, warm and inoffensive would spring instantly to mind. But this was not yet that day, so Erin got the equivalent of a paper jam in her mouth. She stood across the table from him, stalled, no part of her functioning properly.

'After work one night, maybe,' he continued. 'Or a coffee on a Sunday morning, if you'd prefer.'

Perhaps she could say, with a charming smile: *Sorry, it's a chromosome thing*. No. That would be all wrong. Or: *So sorry, but I like girls*. How twee. Maybe: *We could have a drink. As friends*. Lame, lame, lame.

'No? It's okay. You can just say no.' His smile was still in place, but losing sincerity around the edges.

'It's not that…Oh, God…It's not that I don't like…It's not you…Oh look, I have to go.'

In the kitchen Erin smacked hasty thanks onto one cheek

of each lovebird and then hurried out the door, shutting herself into the dark of the late-night street. She tugged on her bulky bouclé coat, and felt in its pockets for a tissue to mop up the mortification that was beginning to leak from her eyes and drip from her nose. But her pockets were empty of everything except a little red rock, just the brush of which against her fingers was enough to remind her of a whole birthday cake full of swaying candle-flames, and of a heart breakingly delicate dusting of icing sugar on a floor.

Tears streaming now, nose running, Erin decided that the whole ocean would be her wishing well, even though she knew that it was only just deep enough to accommodate all the enormous and contradictory wishes (to forget, to remember, to change herself to fit the world, to have the world change to fit her) that were summed up in the shape of that little stone. She walked past her house and all the way to the edge of the city, where she found the tide high and lapping against its concrete retainer. She took the rock out of her pocket and threw it as far as she could out into the grey and weedy waters.

CHRISTINE

Christine wondered how long it would take for this little phase of hers to pass. At least, she assumed that it was a phase, because for a long time — up until about a month ago — she had been quite indifferent to him. Hopefully, she would soon return to that state and be able to look back on this little episode like something in black and white, drained of its intensity. As it was, however, she spent her days struggling to push her thoughts of him to the back of her mind, only to have them spring back into the foreground at the slightest provocation. She did not think that it could get very much worse, and she hoped this meant that it was almost over.

One of the reasons it was so confusing was that he started it. He was the one who invited her for coffee at the bakery around the corner from work. The time she went there with him was the first time she'd been, although she'd heard of the place, and knew that a lot of the younger ones went there in their lunchbreaks. And indeed, on that day, other people from work were there, clustered in telling little groups of two and three. It seemed a place where alliances were made, confirmed and announced, and where gossip could prove as warm and yeasty as the bread dough itself. 'Did you see Luke there with *Christine*?' she could imagine them saying. 'She's got to have fifteen *years* on him.' But he had been willing to be seen there with her. It had been his idea for God's sake. That was what made it so strange.

She had not — well, she didn't think she had — leapt upon him with the appetite of a woman starved of sex and attention for the best part of a decade. She had been friendly. Open. Forthcoming. Perhaps mildly flirtatious, but only to the point of conducting herself in the slightly arch manner that she remembered being effective with men. And he had been friendly, open, forthcoming and possibly mildly flirtatious, too. Or she thought he had. But just the very next day, he had appeared discomfited, alarmed almost, by her repeat performance of friendliness.

Time had passed, but nothing had become clearer. She was simply unable to get him into focus. On some days he seemed alarmingly close, like one's own nose in a magnifying mirror, and on others he seemed to retract into the distance, right out to a place where she had to squint to see that he was actually there. And so, she was confused.

JULIA

In the evenings, Julia walked along the waterfront. Walking and yoga were the only forms of exercise that she could bear and she was trusting that they would be enough to ward off the dire consequences that were said to await women living sedentary, office-bound lives. She walked by the edge of the esplanade's retaining wall when the tide was high, and when the tide was low she stepped down onto the beach, towing her long shadow over its detritus and sand. She was on nodding terms with an elderly, tweed-capped gentleman who stood patiently, at the weed-line on low tide evenings, holding a plastic bag while his black labrador tucked its bum into a defecatory curtsey.

While Julia walked, she played in her mind the short film festival of a feel-good future. Usually, she screened the film about the charming all-rounder of a husband who comes home from rock-climbing practice just in time to baste the Sunday roast; and then she would follow it up with the one about the downy-scalped infant nestling at her milk-full breast. After this, she would return home feeling relaxed and uncoiled (suspecting, though, that the term 'displacement activity' might come up in any scientific assessment of her pleasure).

A few nights after the television program on the science of lust, Julia walked, ducking her head against the wind and watching her boots sink into the soft sand. Just ahead of her a wave receded, its curving edge drawing back like a lace curtain against the sand. And there, amid plain brown pebbles and half-crushed shells, was a small heart-shaped stone. Julia was not even the type to see animals in the clouds, let alone omens in the intertidal zone. She knew that it was just a rock whose shape was the result of various random geological events and a substantial amount of wave action. And yet, she picked it up and gloved its dark redness into the pocket of her coat. When she got home, she took it out and placed it on the table beside her bed.

CHRISTINE

It wasn't the fact that she was so much older than him that prevented Christine from settling the matter out in the open. Thankfully there was another, related issue that she could hold up in front of the age one, successfully obscuring it. And that was that she was in a position of authority. Not specifically over him, but it was a fine line. And there had been lately on the news a particularly troubling example of an abuse of authority. A pretty, young female teacher had found herself in court after becoming sexually involved with a number of her seventeen-year-old male students. Of course, once it was revealed that the number of complainants was seven, the media swiftly dubbed her 'Snow White'. (The headline, incidentally, was SEVEN LITTLE MEN FOR FILTHY SNOW.)

There was one part of Christine which thought the seventeen-year-olds probably enjoyed it and that Snow White was no more than a silly, irresponsible girl who'd had unprecedented access to young, stiff cocks. But as soon as she made a simple transposition of gender, she saw how dodgy this perception became. She tried to imagine herself saying, if the teacher had been a young man, 'Look, the girls probably *enjoyed* it.' She did not even want to contemplate a reversal of her subsequent point about unprecedented access. But what if the equation concerning Luke and her were reversed?

She thought on this, viewing every moment of contact through an inverted lens. She saw her eager friendliness, and his alarmed withdrawal on the day after they had been out for coffee. And suddenly she was revealed to herself as the owner of the uninvited hand pinching the ripe young bottom, as the desperate groper who was pitied and derided behind the closed door of the tearoom. Not only that, but the one whose advances he felt compelled to tolerate because of her seniority, her authority. *Oh my God*, she realised, *I'm the classic old perv*. The thought disgusted and unnerved her. And so for weeks she evaded him, giving him a wide berth in the corridors, replying curtly to his queries and even pretending not to notice him standing in the lift. And then, once he had stepped out of the lift, she would feel foolish, and wonder how a highly paid professional, respected in her field, had inadvertently re-enrolled in the sexual politics of high school.

*

JULIA

One morning, in the hours just before she woke, Julia found the film about the roast-basting husband playing in her dreams. It must have been set a few years before the one about the downy-scalped infant, because once the roast was basted and safely in the oven, the husband took off his apron and took her to bed. He was handsome, this husband, but just slightly lopsidedly so. He had the pectoral muscles of a rock-climber and light brown hair that jutted out in small, endearing tufts. As the credits were rolling, Julia woke up, convinced that she had just had an orgasm in her sleep, and reached over to take the vitamin tablets laid out on the table beside her bed.

Being good at delaying gratification, Julia always took the largest capsule first, followed by the two smaller, easier-to-swallow ones. On this day, the largest capsule caught just a little more painfully than usual at the back of her throat, but it was not until she looked over and saw her usual trio of vitamin tablets still resting by the base of her beside lamp that she realised that what she had swallowed was not a vitamin tablet, but the red heart-shaped rock.

Because of her belief that there was nothing to be gained from panic or haste, Julia did not act immediately. She decided that unless something symptomatic happened in the meantime, she would not go to see her GP before the following morning. Twenty-four hours seemed to her a nice sensible stretch of time. By then, the crisis may simply have, well, *passed*.

But when Julia visited her GP the following morning, the matronly Indian doctor was cross with her.

'You should have come in straightaway,' she scolded with a pointed finger.

'I didn't think it could be too serious. It went down easily enough.'

'The oesophagus is insensible after a certain point,' the GP said, and Julia felt that this was a criticism being levelled at her in her entirety and not only her swallowing apparatus.

Julia was sent for an X-ray, which revealed the rock to be settled on the floor of her stomach. The next day she presented herself at the hospital where she was shown an endoscope loaded up with fibre-optic cabling and a small claw of the hopeful type you might see in an arcade game.

'I'm sorry,' the doctor told her, after the procedure. 'It's passed on from your stomach. We'll have to go at it from the other direction.'

After two days of emptying her body of solid matter and taking her nourishment from transparent things like consommé and jelly, Julia presented herself at the hospital again. She waited, a sheet over her undressed lower half, for another doctor and another probe.

'I'm sorry,' the doctor told her when she woke from a light anaesthetic with a slightly stretched-feeling sphincter. 'Too high for us, I'm afraid.'

'Oh for God's sake. What now?'

The doctor squiggled a mouth, a stomach and a bowel onto his drug company desk pad.

'Your little friend is most likely at the ileocaecal junction,' he said, making emphatic circles with his ballpoint. 'The obvious risk is that it will block movement through your bowel altogether. But the other risk is that it will push through and do some damage to the tissue on the way. You could even end up with a bowel perforation and, trust me, you don't want to go there. You've heard the term peritonitis? Rather common on death certificates early last century.'

Perforation. Julia thought of the dotted line above a payment slip: tear here.

'I'm in court tomorrow,' she said, aware of both her petulant tone and its misplacement. 'It's not a case I can pass over.'

'Well, we can't take the risk of waiting until Monday, so I'd be pushing to get you to the surgeon by Friday at the latest. That's the fourteenth.'

Thought Julia: *Well, Happy Valentine's Day to me.*

CHRISTINE

Christine's predecessor had liked the fact that it was called a theatre. It hadn't mattered to him that the curtains were green instead of black. He'd had a handful of nurses to serve as both audience and supporting cast and he'd played it like a comedy, turning up the symphonies on Classic FM and conducting the orchestras with mischievous inflections of his bootbrush-bristle eyebrows. Christine preferred to concentrate in silence and she knew that the nurses found her conscientiously dull by comparison.

In theatre this particular Friday, the scout to the scrubbed nurse was Sister Luke Boyles. Christine was physically aware of his proximity as she stood at the operating table making her opening incision.

'This is the one with the rock?' he asked.

No one can say she doesn't swallow, she thought. And then she flushed: *Oh God, I belong on the* Benny Hill Show.

She hooked out a segment of ropey bowel and felt along it for the obstruction. Then she made a small slice down the length of tubular tissue and squeezed a small hard lump out into her hand. Fingering away a light coating of greeny-yellow bile, she found a little heart lying blood red in her palm. She fancied that she saw it pulse.

'Got 'im,' said Luke. 'Good darts, doctor.'

Christine looked up and tried to identify his expression judging by the rectangle of face between his mop hat and surgical mask. It was impossible to be certain, but she had a strong feeling that there was a wolfish grin going on behind the pleated gauze. She flushed again, hotter and brighter this time, as he closed one eye in a slow, deliberate wink.

For just a heartbeat, she considered flicking the stone to him across the torso of her anaethetised patient, and watching him catch it in a swift, latex grip. 'Happy Valentine's Day,' she would say flippantly. Ironically. Just a bit of medical humour. The intent of which could be easily denied.

Then she remembered the image of an old man's unwelcome fingers on a young woman's firm-fleshed tush. And thought of Snow White in her prison cell, who would remember only with her own searching fingers the pleasures of her seven young playmates. She gestured briskly to Luke to pass her the specimen jar that sat, its yellow lid already removed, on the instrument table. And very deliberately, she did not meet his eye as the rock hit the bottom of it with a small, disappointed *tink*.

LOSS

The True Daughter

I

'Kate,' says Faye, 'is a mezzosoprano. For which I am grateful, actually.'

There is opera playing, and it seems to Tamsin to occupy Faye's apartment as if it were part of the décor, the rich voice echoing the timber of the furniture, rippling over near-white carpet as soft as the fleece of a newborn lamb.

'I suspect sopranos are flightier, altogether more given to tantrums and putting on airs and graces. I don't see how it can possibly be good for your equilibrium, spending all that time in the upper registers. Also, sopranos are invariably blonde.'

Tamsin smiles. It is the morning of her first day and already she thinks that she will like Faye. She does not, however, think that she will like Kate. Tamsin suspects her to be the sort of daughter who will leave it until the very end. Then she will jet in, all European couture and big sunglasses, just in time to perform a day or two of lower-register histrionics and take the starring role at the funeral. Most likely, she will be the type to treat her mother's nurses like so many hired hands, dispatching them to the kitchen for more tea, or to the bathroom for more tissues. Kate, Tamsin can already tell, will be the sort of woman to make her feel, keenly, the girlishness of her plain brown ponytail.

It hardly matters, since it is more or less everywhere now, where it began. But when Tamsin undresses Faye for her sponge bath, the origin is clear. Beneath the bodice of her nightgown Faye's chest, without its breasts, is as profoundly nude as an unfeathered baby bird. Tamsin sponges over the buckled scarring, gently, apologising to the skin for the indignities it has already suffered.

'They were rather nice, you know. I didn't know that, of course, when I had them,' Faye says as Tamsin buttons up the front of a clean gown. 'Still, at least I passed on their likeness to Kate.'

Tamsin draws up a vial of morphia and stretches out the bone and fine hide of Faye's arm. A brisk slap to the arm's crook and the needle slips unnoticed into the still-stinging skin.

'That barely hurt at all,' Faye says and Tamsin cannot prevent the corners of her mouth from turning up, just a little.

'There is a bit of an art to it,' she admits.

In the afternoon Faye sleeps, opera turned down low. Her bed is in the front room now, along with all of her paintings. The rest of the apartment has a ransacked look, picture hooks hanging bare on cream walls marked by faint rectangles of absence.

Cluttered together on two large windowless walls, the paintings make a jigsaw puzzle gallery, just inches between their frames. When Tamsin looks closely, she finds that she knows them already. Almost. She knows their shapes and colours, but not their precise configurations. She looks until she understands that they are painters' *other* works; the equivalent, perhaps, of photographs taken a few moments before or after the perfect shot. Tamsin stands for a long time before a melon-breasted, tangle-limbed nude who reclines by a window filled with the ultramarine of Sydney Harbour, and decides that Faye has taste, as well as money.

She thinks that she will like this job. As always, she doesn't know how long it will last, but it is better paid than most. If she is disciplined about setting some of her wages aside, perhaps it will not be so much of a struggle next time to make it through the weeks or months before someone else begins in earnest to die, and can afford the luxury of doing it in their own home. She had tried not to look pleasantly surprised when Faye's nephew, who had interviewed her for the job, named his price. Impressed by her references, he had brought her into this room to meet Faye, and she remembers now how all the while that they talked his eyes caressed the walls.

At the end of the day Tamsin leaves Faye in the care of the night nurse and rides home on her bike. There is a quicker way but Tamsin does not take it. Even here, out on the far edge of the arcing route she follows, she can feel the pull of the place she is avoiding. It has become a gaping hole in the outskirts of her city, a swirling plughole of orange bricks, which threatens to suck in first the neighbouring buildings, then the architecture of the surrounding blocks, then the suburbs in concentric rings until the spiralling devastation reaches out as far as the small weatherboard house where Tamsin lives, not happily anymore, with Michael.

II

'Kate,' says Faye, 'has true auburn hair. The sort of hair I would rather have liked for myself, I confess.'

Tamsin can imagine this true auburn hair — long, loosely curling, sweeping back from Kate's dramatic face. She pictures Kate with the square, capacious jaw of a diva and a chin perpetually upthrust. In her publicity photos she would wear deep green velvet, a portrait neckline gesturing down to the healthy flesh of her breasts.

'She was a wonderful Cenerentola, when she was younger. She does Rosina well, too, but it's Orfeo that she's known for.'

'Orfeo?'

'As in Orpheus. Pants role. The soprano plays Euridice.'

'Tragic ending, I assume.'

'Actually Gluck has Amor, the god of love, take pity on Orfeo and bring Euridice back to life in the final act.'

'That was generous of him.'

'I suspect he felt it was only fair to finish with a big chorus and some swooning,' she says. And then she giggles. 'I must bear that in mind myself.'

Faye's giggle is one of the things Tamsin likes most about

her. It is a delighted, girlish giggle, and far from being at odds with her old woman's face, it gives purpose to every crease. When Faye giggles, Tamsin does too. She has never known anyone to approach death so cheerfully, as if it were just a thing she had never got around to doing before.

By the end of her first week with Faye, Tamsin is riding home by a still-longer route, widening her circle of avoidance. It leads her through a suburb she has never before had reason to visit, down a short street with cafés and shops full of inessential and expensive things. Women whom she suspects are doctors' wives return to glossy cars with armloads of flowers.

She stands by the window of a small boutique, guilty and furtive. She looks in and sees, browsing through racks of tiny clothes, women whose peculiarly shaped bodies show that they have nothing to hide. Tamsin thinks of the babies inside them, plump as broad beans, securely attached to their vines. If these women looked at her, Tamsin wonders, would they know? Could they tell? Is there a mark? Does it show? She waits until the shop is empty of customers before she enters. She buys a hat, in the very smallest size. It is white. She does not know enough to choose something pink or blue.

Wits about her, Tamsin rides through fumy, traffic-thick streets. She thinks of her house, which will already be occupied by Michael; his university books open on the kitchen table, his cooking in the pot. She takes a detour and cycles twice around a lake whose still surface reflects the darkening sky.

III

'Kate,' says Faye, 'married well. She took my advice on that matter. I told her to look not for an adversary, but for a rock.'

Tamsin supposes that when Kate does appear, it will be with this husband-of-Gibraltar in obedient tow. She makes a mental note to check whether or not his jumper is the same colour as his wife's ensemble of suitcases.

'And I told her that it would be best if he were tone deaf, too. That way he could only ever admire her, and never be tempted to criticise.'

Tamsin doesn't know whether Faye's advice to her daughter on the subject of husbands was the result of Faye having herself married an adversary or a rock, someone who was tone deaf or someone who had a tendency to criticise. She would like to know, but it is not her way to ask questions of her patients. In part this is because she is a nurse whose task it is to bring ease, not to prod at what might turn out to be invisible bruises. But it is also because she finds it less interesting to engage in the anxious, hasty excavation of inquiry than to wait and see which fragments of a life — here at life's end — are the ones her patients consider important enough to share.

At the end of her first month, Tamsin knows only that Faye's husband was a surgeon. Called Keith. She does not yet know how long ago, or from what, he died. But she does think it makes sense that Faye was a doctor's wife. She has the well-preserved look of a woman with the twin luxuries of money and time. Tamsin has leafed through the petite and pristine outfits hanging in Faye's wardrobe, and slipped her hand up inside a sheath of drycleaner's plastic to touch the as-new red velvet of a hooded opera cape. She has seen, nesting in the compartments of a complex timber grid beneath the hanging clothes, a large (but not obscenely large) number of shoes. Their soles are only lightly scratched, and the silks, satins, leathers and suedes of their uppers are creased only as much as would indicate careful wear. The same might be said of Faye's complexion.

Tamsin is chastened by Faye's personal habits. It is rare for her to drink anything other than water with a squeeze of lemon juice. She eats delicately, too: small plates of fig and passionfruit drizzled with just a little honey and plain yoghurt, undressed salads of rocket, pecan and pear. She tells Tamsin that she never cooks; she only buys fresh food that will look pleasing on a plate. This is what she tells Tamsin, and then she reminds herself, with a giggle, that she must consign this sentence to the past tense.

Each night Tamsin sleeps next to Michael in a bed beneath which is a suitcase. Because Michael has no curiosity, Tamsin has no need to lock it, even though it now contains things that she does not want him to see. On nights when he studies late at the library, she unpacks its contents onto the bed. She lays out the small white singlets, the small white hats, mittens and socks. And then she puts them away again.

Most nights Michael gets into bed beside her and kisses her, with intent. And she kisses him back, without. And he takes up his book from the bedside table without asking why, or why not. She wishes that he would ask, because she has the answer ready. It is right there, just behind her bottom teeth, where she could oh-so-easily flick it up and onto her tongue. It's tainted, she would say, if only he would ask. Tarnished. She would give him words to conjure the metallic sheen of her spilled blood under bright lights.

IV

'Where is Kate?'

As time passes, this is the question Tamsin begins to carry with her up and down the aisles of supermarkets, stir into her pasta sauce, and squeeze onto her toothbrush late at night. It is the question that flares on the day that Faye's femur crumbles like plaster of Paris beneath the weight of her pelvis, the very last day of her life that she is able to stand on her feet. It steadily burns as weeks pass and Tamsin measures Faye's decline against the black-lined fractions of the syringes she draws up and plunges into needle-bruised skin. It will not be long now. And the telephone does not ring.

'You don't have any photos on display,' Tamsin observes one day.

'I like my pictures to be made of paint.'

'You must at least have some pictures of Kate.'

'I brought her into the world. Her face is the one I am least in danger of forgetting.'

It is one of the worst things for Tamsin: that the face she never saw is unrecoverable. Resentment snakes through her, a drug in her veins. It is general, indiscriminate. Kate may have been the only one ever to have curled up inside Faye's body, but she, Tamsin, will be the one to share the final intimacies of her life. She will give the needles that dull the pain, place the pillows that cushion the hollows of her body, wipe the shit from her shrivelled arse. She will be the true daughter at the end.

V

'Where is Kate?' is the question Tamsin wants to ask Faye. She asks Michael instead, and his answers turn into a game.

'Perhaps she's a suburban drunk with nine grotty kids and she smokes fag butts from ashtrays at shopping centres.'

'Perhaps she's taken a vow of silence in a Mongolian yurt.'

'Perhaps she lives in a trailer park in Texas with a Mormon polygamist and his six other wives.'

'Perhaps she's not Kate anymore, but Kevin.'

A Word from Rosie Little
ON NOMINATIVE DETERMINISM

We've all heard jokes like the one about the Greek skydiver, Con Descending, but the creepy regularity with which people's names match their vocations or characteristics is no laughing matter to me. I am certain that the entire responsibility for my failure to grow beyond five feet can be sheeted home to my unfortunate family name. Just how its six letters have managed to entirely counter the effects of fresh genes injected into the Little family pool over successive generations I don't know, but I do know that the quip 'Little by name, little by nature' wore out its welcome with me well before I attained the long-coveted height at which I could graduate from the booster seat in the back of my mother's car.

The naming game began with Adam, apparently, who got to decide how to refer to all the bits and pieces God left lying around for him in the garden. Later on, explorers seemed to get quite a kick out of naming things too. But these days, unless you're a botanist and can find a particularly obscure orchid, or you're an astronomer with a telescope powerful enough to track down a new star, the only things you're likely to get to name are your pets and your kids. So, if you feel the desire come upon you to fling names around like a seventeenth-century sea captain, you'll need to have a particularly large family, or buy yourself a substantial aquarium and stock it with a great many fish.

What's in a name? A Rosie by any other might smell as sweet, but would I have grown into precisely the same girl if my parents had called me Persephone? It's such a gamble. Do you give your child a fanciful name in the hope that it will give them a head start in marking themselves out from the flock? Or do you take the opposite approach and give them a plain name, upon which they might write whichever personality they choose? I think I'd lean towards supplying a child with a distinctive brand, but I know that it can go horribly wrong. It certainly did for one babe whose birth notice I read recently. Perhaps her parents envisaged her growing up to unlock the complex ciphers of cyberspace, but I suspect it's more likely that she'll spend her life trying to work out why on earth her parents called her 'Decoda'.

But then, it doesn't necessarily follow that a person with a good, sensible name will be a good, sensible person. Even if it is a no-nonsense, easy-to-spell, no-tricks name like Kate.

*

Then one night he says, 'Perhaps it's not Kate that's the dark horse. Perhaps it's Faye. Maybe she murdered Kate and buried her beneath the hydrangeas.'

His stupidity wakes every sleeping thing inside of her and in an instant Tamsin can hear the thrumming and drumming of a thousand demons' tiny veined wings in her chest. Within three moves the conversation is a fight and soon he is saying it again: 'It wasn't the right time, love. We talked about this. My degree. Financially, we —'

And she is getting shriller as she moves through her lines: '*Financially* we killed our child so we could afford a nice house for our child to live in. We killed our baby so one day we could send it to a private school, so it could wear nice clothes. How does any of this make sense to you?'

He doesn't pull the punchline: 'Tam, it was a decision we made together.'

And she hates him, hates him, for saying it. Most of all because it is true. She hates him all the way up the stairs to the bedroom, and for all of the time it takes to get out of her clothes and get into the shower. She wants to wash from her mind the orange-bricked building and its lay-back chair and its plughole swirling with her own red cells. Standing in the hot fall she feels an invisible cat kneading at her abdomen. Since the termination her periods have been clotty and painful. Now blood begins to fall from between her legs in heavy splotches. It is claret, then pink, as the diluting water swirls it towards the plughole.

After a while Michael opens the shower door, his look concerned, gentle. It makes her want to stretch her wet arms around him and pull him, clothes and all, into the shower with her. She wishes the droplets were her tears, and that he would stand in them until he was drenched. Then she sees him see the blood and she sees him think a thought he is too well-schooled to say out loud. But he doesn't have to say it. The damage is done. In place of concern there is relief — twofold. His mouth tightens into a tiny patronising smile, and she wishes her hands were of the type that could flick out a set of long sharp claws with which to scratch his face. She slams the shower door, catching his fingers, and when she sees through the beaded glass how he clutches them in pain, she is glad.

VI

'Where is Kate?' Tamsin finally asks Faye, on a day when her bitterness is so strong that she cannot help but make everyone else taste it too.

She asks her question with a careful measure of spite, her eyes on the face of her fob watch and her fingertips pressed firmly into the old woman's wrist. She expects to feel the pulse leap in concert with her own. But it does not.

'She's in the liquor cabinet.'

Tamsin flushes, hot with guilt. She has been cruel. And not only that, she has been cruel to an old woman whose mind — her sharp and beautiful mind — is following her body into decay. Tamsin has nursed more than one person through and beyond this point, but she had not thought that it would happen to Faye.

'In the liquor cabinet? I see.'

'That mollifying tone does not become you, you know.'

Tamsin looks away from the watch face, losing count, to find Faye's eyes as clear as ever.

'And that crazy old biddy one doesn't do much for you. You frightened me.'

'The anger goes, darling. I can promise you that much. It is the most volatile part, and it soon burns itself off.'

Tamsin flinches as if slapped. She had not known it could be seen from the outside.

'And then,' says Faye, 'there is only the sadness.'

VII

'Kate,' says Faye, 'really is in the liquor cabinet, you know.'

And on this day, which feels like one of the very last they will spend together, Tamsin is almost ready to believe her.

'You can take her out if you want to. I haven't taken her out for years.'

'So you have got a photo of her?'

'Go on. At the back.'

'Why wouldn't you show me before?'

'Behind the port.'

The ownership of a liquor cabinet is, to Tamsin — whose meagre supply of cheap booze sits in the corner of her kitchen cupboard — an index of elegance. A woman who owns a liquor cabinet is surely one who can coil her hair into a chignon and tong out lemon wedges with a demeanour as cool as the ice in her silver bucket. Tamsin imagines a young Faye, shaped like a *Vogue* paper pattern sketch, handing out drinks at a party.

The cabinet's rosewood doors open in her hands like those of an expensive car, smooth and substantial. Inside is the cut crystal of several decanters fitted with orbed stoppers. There is ruby port, sapphire gin, and something poisonously emerald. Tamsin removes the stopper and puts her nose to the neck.

'Crème de menthe? Yuck. Honestly Faye. And here I was thinking you had perfect taste.'

'At the back, at the back.'

And at the back, behind the port, Tamsin sees Kate.

Kate is small. Much smaller than Tamsin would have expected. Hers is a thick glass jar with the word *Fowlers* pressed into the metal of its lid. Inside she floats, her delicate infant skin faintly rippled by the liquid preservative. Away from her belly twists a length of purplish flex, an umbilical cord to nowhere.

'Oh, Faye.'

'Born too early, you see. Much too early. There was nothing that could be done.'

Tamsin touches a fingertip to the glass, as if she might trace the sculpted curves of the baby's tiny lips, or the sparse pale hairs of her eyebrows.

'I'd wanted her so much, I couldn't bear to leave the hospital without her. Keith arranged it for me, knew who to speak to. When I brought her home, I didn't know where to put her. The liquor cabinet seemed somehow…ironic. When happiness is no longer possible, you see, one might as well try to keep oneself amused.'

Tamsin is gentle, but when she lifts the jar she cannot prevent the foetus from bobbing stiffly in her formalin bath, knees and elbows fending glass.

'Let me see her.'

Tamsin cradles Kate in her arms for a moment before handing her to her mother, propped on the pillows of her bed. Faye takes her tenderly and when her tears fall, they touch glass, dissolving into its thickness.

VIII

'Kate,' Tamsin thinks.

It is the first thing she thinks on the day she arrives to find the apartment's front door, its windows and the rear of an ambulance left gapingly, indecently, open. It could almost be Faye's frail corpse so carelessly exposed. Tamsin ditches her bike on the street and rushes, wanting desperately to draw a nightgown down over the whole, horrible scene.

The night nurse is on the patio, smoking and looking out over the river, her long ribbed cardigan tightly twisted around her torso. Faye's nephew is there too, but he cannot settle to sitting or standing or leaning. His movements criss-cross the near-white carpet but avoid the men in blue coveralls who have clipboards and kind faces. They have already moved Faye out of her own bed and onto the hard and narrow mattress of the ambulance trolley.

Tamsin touches the now slightly yellowed skin of her face, smoothes the soft lilac of her hair. The nephew watches as if Tamsin were television.

'She liked you.'

'I liked her.'

'Thank you. For making her comfortable.'

Tamsin lifts Faye's bird-bone hand and touches the back of it to her cheek. She lays it down again and nods to the ambulance officer who clicks off the brakes and begins to wheel the trolley towards the door.

'She wanted you to have something,' the nephew tells Tamsin. 'She said you could choose.'

Tamsin wonders if he knows how obviously his eyes flicker to the smallest of the paintings, the ones he is not sure she knows are the most valuable of all. So easily could she claim one, *just a small one*, and all in the guise of being too modest to pick a larger canvas.

'Anything. She did say anything.'

Tamsin sees how he must fight himself to say this, and by what a narrow margin his better self wins.

'Could I have one of the decanters, from the liquor cabinet?'

'A decanter? Good God, you can have the lot.'

IX

'Kate,' Tamsin answers the woman making expert tucks in tissue paper on the counter.

'Short for Katherine?'

'No. Just Kate.'

'How lovely to hear a nice *plain* name. Almost unusual nowadays, isn't it? And how old?"

'Twelve…yes, twelve months.'

'Oh you do have to think, don't you? Goes so quickly. Before you know it, they're asking for the car keys.'

Twelve months. Can it really have been so long? Tamsin has not the usual milestones — sitting, crawling, standing, walking — to help her keep track.

'Twelve months,' the woman says, clucking her tongue. 'Oh, they're gorgeous at that age, aren't they? Well, I'm sure your little Kate will look adorable in these.'

They are shoes, this time, of the softest pink leather.

Tamsin checks her watch. Now that Michael is working again, there is no need to rush. There is plenty of time yet, before he gets home, to add to her accumulation of secrets in the suitcase beneath the bed. In the street she sits at an outdoor café table and watches the movements of doctors' wives and flowers and glossy cars. Into the boutique from which she has just come, go women with loose shirts over growing bellies. But Tamsin does not envy them. Not anymore.

DESTINY

Rosie Little Joins the Dots

....

I t is all very well to dream of climbing through the ceiling of a newspaper office via the branching ladder of an overgrown pot plant, out into the starry night sky. But even if you elect to take a more sensible approach — tender your resignation in warm and regretful terms, work out your notice, and leave through the front door on a Friday afternoon after a few paper cups of cask moselle — you still find yourself as bewildered as if you really were adrift on a rooftop, staring into the benignly unhelpful face of the Town Clock, with nothing more than a Mini with a busted door, twenty-seven pairs of red shoes and an arts degree to your name, wondering what on earth to do next.

I went to see Eve.

'What's it like?' I asked her, part way through the third bottle of wine, having invoked the privileges of dear friendship and rare appearance in order to keep her up drinking long past the hour Adam had excused himself and gone to bed.

'What?' she asked sleepily.

'All this,' I said, waving my hand to take in the new and tasteful expanses of the remodelled picker's hut, the room where her calm and dependable husband lay in his half of the marital bed, the nursery where their little boys were twinned in deep sleep and rude good health, the pair of matching dogs as flat as rugs before the open fire, and the walls ripely hung with painted apples. 'You always were five steps ahead of me, Evie.'

'That depends entirely, dear girl, on which direction you're headed.'

'But where do I go *now*?'

She threw a cushion at me. 'Go to sleep, for God's sake. I'm up to my neck in toddler shit in two and a half hours.'

A few weeks later, I set sail.

Although, I find 'sail' to be a curious verb for the action of the floating white American skyscraper upon whose luxurious decks I stood as I pinned to my lapel the shining name tag that bore the legend ASSISTANT PURSER ROSIE LITTLE.

Oh please, admire me in my cruise company uniform: the snug-fitting bottle-green skirt, the matching fitted jacket, the nylon nanna-print blouse, the beige pantyhose (that I ripped through at the startling rate of one pair every two days due to a ridiculous propensity for snagging), and the sensibly low-heeled bottle-green pumps. And please, do reach into the breast pocket of my jacket and bring out, for your amusement and mine, the laminated card which I could (and did) get a written reprimand for failing to carry, and upon which are printed the ten commandments of my life aboard the vessel. My favourites were always Number Three: 'I smile, I am on stage', and Number Ten: 'I never say no. I say "I will be pleased to check and see"'.

I shared my flimsy walled, lower deck cabin with a Texan called Beth. Although she quite possibly had to have the pom-poms surgically removed from her cheerleader wrists before she took up her job as a shipboard dancer, she was forthright and funny and we were friends in an instant. Her boyfriend, also a dancer, was a Mexican called Octavio, whose polished manner and industrial strength hairdo remained undented even after a full day of cha-cha-chaing the wibbly flesh of seventy-year-old Nebraskan matrons.

'Octavio is the only man in the world who would take his girlfriend on an outing to Tiffany's to show her the ring that he's going to buy for *himself*,' was Beth's favourite of her stock complaints about Octavio, all of which she would deliver with a 360-degree roll of her wide eyes and follow with a full-lung-capacity sigh.

If you have ever been a passenger on a cruise ship, then you will know that there are diversions scheduled on the half-hour, at least. There are dance lessons in a variety of styles, cooking classes, ice sculpture demonstrations, investment seminars, nature talks, and auctions of the kind of art that is designed to pick out the colours in your curtain fabric. But not one of these activities is more favoured by the American retirees — who come aboard in order to fully exercise the hard-earned privileges of a lifetime of work in the family carpet/rubber/plastics /44-foot motorhome business — than the activity in which it was my thankless task to accommodate them: complaining. Some might disagree with me, and put forward the view that *eating* is more popular even than complaining. But I always found it difficult to think of eating as a discrete activity when — much like blinking — it was something that passengers seemed subconsciously to be doing whenever they were awake.

As a passenger on a cruise ship you may, three times a day, take your designated seat in the Emerald Court dining room and order anything on the menu. You may order *everything* on the menu. And since the food is included in the overall price of the cruise, this is precisely what you do. You order six plates of food and take two mouthfuls from each, retaining room, of course, for whichever dessert the pyromaniac of a chef is flambéing on that particular day. Should you miss a meal, or get peckish, you can dine out any old time at the pizzeria, or call into the patisserie for a snack. And should you be on deck in the deep night of an ocean crossing, you might be lucky enough to see the ship perform a moonlit excretion: a colossal tide of waste food mingling with an equally colossal tide of human shit in a gleaming, spreading slick.

I spent a year in bottle-green uniform. And then another. Pulling into port at dawn, setting sail for somewhere else at dusk, I gathered the seaside cities of the world in postcard-sized impressions. From behind the smooth curve of my reception-area desk, I fielded complaints about the standard of toilets in war-torn nations and the unacceptable wait for the between-decks elevators. I pacified indignant passengers returning from shore excursions having learned that not every shopowner on the planet provides change in American dollars. Occasionally I was let out to join a shore excursion, ostensibly as an interpretive guide, but actually as a shepherd for our white-haired and woolly-brained charges.

I tolerated as best I could my English and chook-bum-mouthed supervisor (whose parents spelled her name 'Natarsha', with the extra 'r', just to be absolutely certain that she sounded like a insufferable prat), who once squeezed me into her cupboard-sized office in order to tick me off for taking three turns, instead of two turns, in the elastic bands that we used for securing the change bags at the end of each day. It was Natarsha who routinely checked that I was carrying my commandment card by asking me to take it out and read to her Number Six: 'I wear proper and safe footwear that is clean and polished, and I wear my name tag', or Number Eight: 'I answer the phone with a smile in my voice', and who filed a formal reprimand with Head Office on the day she caught me without the commandments in my pocket.

As for the Love Boat? Ha! The old saying was true: the only people who took cruises were the overfed, the newlywed and the nearly dead. And for two years, my romantic adventures went no further than the vicarious enjoyment of Beth and Octavio's turbulent tango, and a mildly flirtatious friendship with a croupier in the onboard casino. Garry was from Adelaide, told the kind of filthy jokes that could only have been scraped off the floor of an Australian pub, and he could kick my arse at the pool table. We each earned ourselves a demerit point when we were caught, in the early hours of the morning, in the passenger-only zone of the on-deck hot tub. It was my second strike, but it was Garry's third.

'One for the road?' he asked, gesturing to his cabin door with a hitchhiking thumb on the night before he was sent home, unemployed.

'Thanks Gaz, for the offer, but "I will be pleased to check and see".'

By the time my two years turned into two and a half, it was summer in the northern hemisphere and the ship was sliding like a big white Monopoly hotel up and down the shattered-diamond coast of Alaska. And as it dodged through dense archipelagos and followed curving bays with mouths full of the bared and aqua-blue teeth of glaciers, both the passengers and Assistant Purser Rosie Little were introduced to a new kind of diversion.

He was older than me — just enough to make me feel younger — but not very much taller, and he came aboard for the season as a visiting writer, to give daily readings in the Top Deck Lounge and to mess up my composure with his speckled, teasing stare.

'Rosie and Russell. Oh, that's cute,' said Beth, when I confessed to the fizz of excitement I'd felt on the day that it had fallen to me to give him a tour of the ship, after which I'd stayed in the back of the lounge to listen to him read in his wiry

Scottish accent a suite of tender poems about bird flight and heartbreak.

'Why cute?' I asked.

She stretched out on her bunk in her pale blue babydoll nightie, and opened a packet of Oreos. Beth was impervious to the gut-lifting sensation of the ship heaving on an ocean swell. I, on the other hand, sat up in bed sipping ginger tea.

'You know,' she said, 'that nominative thing you're always talking about.'

'Nominative determinism? What do you mean? Why cute?'

'Look up "Russell",' she said, flinging me the baby name book that she kept in her bedside drawer and used for the purpose of making long lists of possible first and middle names for the children she was sure she would one day have with Octavio.

'Ruben, Rudolph, Rupert…here we go…Russell: the colour red, or red-haired one,' I read out.

'See? Rose Red meets her man!'

'Beth,' I said, closing the book and running a finger down its spine, 'that actually is a bit weird. Because guess what his last name is?'

'What?'

'Short.'

'No way! Rosie Little and Russell Short? Oh my God,' she said. 'You two are MFEO.'

'What?'

'Oh, c'mon. *Made* For Each Other.'

*

Russell Short and I began to spend a lot of time together and, for me, the conversation we shared was like an exotic banquet after years of white bread. It was both sweet and piquant, full of allusion and quotation, and it was almost enough to mend my difficult relationship with the word 'eclectic'. It was a conversation that required footnotes, too, and one that had me up late at night in the ship's library, cracking open the untouched leather of a fine dictionary to look up words like 'deliquesce', or hunting on the internet for the rest of an Emily Dickinson poem, with the opening lines of which — 'Nobody knows this little Rose/It might a pilgrim be' — he would quite often greet me.

And so we flirted, up and down the Alaskan coast, until one day when we were on deck, sipping scotch chilled with ice chips from the hunk of glacier that Russell had brought back from a walk in the mountains, and he said, 'You know, we're playing a game, you and I.'

His words gave me a little jolt, making me think that he was about to say something dangerously real. But when I looked over at him for a cue, he seemed perfectly calm.

'We are?'

'Yes, we are playing a game. But we are only playing it in our minds. Do you want to play for real?'

'For real?' I asked, wishing I had the faintest clue what he meant.

'Well? Do you?'

'I don't know. What's the name of this game?'

'The name of this game is Not Pushing the Glass off the Table,' he said, downing his scotch and crunching the last shard of ice between his teeth.

'And what are the rules of Not Pushing the Glass off the Table?'

'Ah, sensible girl. A cautious approach,' he said, inverting his tumbler.

It was one of the kind that tapers into a hexagon of cut panels and he placed it upside down on the table, close to the edge.

'The aim of the game is to see how far you can push the glass without actually pushing it off,' he explained, and pushed the glass until a slender crescent of its rim extended over the edge of the tabletop.

'Now your turn,' he invited.

'Like so?' I asked, moving the glass only a fraction.

'Oh come on. It's only your first go. Fortune favours the bold.'

'Is that better?'

'Passable,' he allowed. 'My turn.'

And turn about, we continued to move the glass, making the crescent grow.

'You see,' he said, tapping the glass forward with his fingertips, 'the wonderful thing about this game is that you can push and nudge the glass towards the edge, but if it falls to the ground and smashes, you always have the consolation that it was most expressly not your intention to break it. Your turn.'

When the amount of unsupported rim was an almost perfect half-circle, I gave the glass a tiny push, stopping just short of the point at which I thought it would begin to teeter.

'I'd say that's it. Right there,' he said. 'That's as close to the edge as that glass will go without falling.'

'You're piking out?'

'You think it can go further?'

'Isn't that what we have to find out?' I asked.

'You've played this game before, haven't you?'

'Your turn,' I invited.

'You're quite sure?'

'Not at all.'

'But you want me to do it anyway?'

'Yes,' I said, giggling.

'And of that you are certain?'

'Go on.'

'No, I forfeit. You do it,' he said.

And I did. I gave the glass one more little push, and when it landed on the deck it did not so much shatter as simply fall into pieces. At our feet were the thick wedge of the glass's base and several triangular shards — isosceles, equilateral — all of them pointing in only one direction.

His cabin had a porthole that was sometimes a circle of blue waves and sometimes a circle of sky. Most times, though, it held the line of the horizon, and as this line moved up and down with the motion of the ship, the porthole appeared to fill and empty with water. As the season progressed, I came to think of that porthole as a kind of spirit level that measured my own equilibrium as I ebbed and flowed in Russell's bunk.

In the lounge, in the dining room, on the deck, he was always older, wiser, worldlier, wordier than me. But I loved the fact that in his cabin, within the white wash of daily-laundered sheets, there were moments of silence in which I could pick up the scent of vulnerability on his naked skin. Or I thought that I could.

'Rose,' he said, one afternoon, as I slowly subsided in his arms.

'Yes?' I said, from where my head lay in the bony hollow of his bare shoulder.

'I should probably tell you that on the last cruise of the season, my wife will be coming aboard.'

'Your *wife*?' I asked, propping myself up to look into his face.

It wore an expression that was quite unconcerned.

'Yes, minikin. My wife,' he said, quite definitely, at the same time as he tenderly fingered my cheek.

'Your *wife*?' I repeated.

He shrugged. 'Oh, Rose, you remember the name of the game,' he said.

'Game?'

'It isn't called Pushing the Glass off the Table,' he said.

Very clever, I thought. I could almost have applauded his immaculate groundwork. For now I knew that even if I were to fall to the ground and smash, right in front of him, he could easily excuse himself with the fact that it was most expressly not his intention to break me.

One Final Word from Rosie Little

On the day that I left school, my favourite English teacher took me aside to give me some parting words of advice. And I remembered her words clearly, even though I did not immediately understand their relevance. It's important, she said, with not the faintest trace of irony in her voice, to know when to use the cake fork.

What was this that she was offering me? A dot point from her nanna's etiquette manual? A titbit of snooty trivia, useful only in the context of high tea at a ladies' service club, or the odd occasion on which one might dine with the governor? Or was it something else entirely?

Now that I have had a few years in which to think on it, I am almost certain that my teacher was speaking to me of words. For is not a precisely or cleverly used word just like a cake fork: a fine and delicately crafted thing, ideally adapted for one specific task? Is not the pleasure of attacking a passionfruit sponge with a dainty silver fork, quite similar to the pleasure one takes from having to hand just the right, exquisitely honed word?

But while it is a joy to have words like

'accismus' and 'stridulate' tucked away in your silver drawer, you would hardly want to use them every day of the week. You can eat cake perfectly politely without recourse to a cake fork, after all. There are times when a dinner fork will do just fine. And there are other times when, even if a cake fork is laid out for you, it is best to ignore it and use your fingers. And there are other times still, when nothing less than a pitchfork will do. The trick, of course, is to know which is which is which.

I think that my schoolteacher's advice is worth passing on, but with an amendment that I made in the light of the filleting I suffered at the hands of the sesquipedalian Russell Short. For cake forks, like other small silvery things — mirrors, flying fish, the tips of some people's tongues — can be deceptive. So to you, I would say it's important to know when to use the cake fork, but it is equally important to know who is using the cake fork on you.

*

Horribly early on the day after Russell Short casually tossed his wife into our post-coital bliss, I sat knees-together on a small, rear-facing seat in a minibus full of cruise passengers. While the automated section of my brain supplied the cheery patter that I delivered into the overheated mouthpiece of a headset, I used the conscious part to wonder if there was one precise word for 'I've taken a king hit from a direction that I did not expect, but even if I had, I could not have known that I would feel so profoundly winded'. If there was such a word, then I couldn't think of it.

The scenery upon which I was commentating was barely visible, only just coming up into greyscale with the creeping dawn. Our passengers were on their way to take a hot-air balloon ride on the soft early-morning air currents, and it was still not fully light when the minibus pulled into a car park where four flaccid but colourful sheaths were slowly inflating upwards from the bitumen. By the side of one of these stood a woman in a white lacy dress, clutching a small white Bible and a posy of white flowers, and a man in a tuxedo, who was nervously clasping and unclasping his hands in front of his crotch.

'Say,' said an elderly gent with huge and stiffly cartilaginous ears, as I helped him down from the bus. 'Are those two going to get married up in one of them hot-air balloons?'

'No,' I said. 'They came to this car park a while back and thought, wow, what a place to tie the knot!'

I caught Natarsha's disapproving look from the far side of the bus door, but it wasn't until later, when I was back aboard the ship and cornered once again in the tiny empire of her office, that I realised how final a mistake I had made.

'Number Ten, Rosie. Number Ten,' she said, filling in the blanks of my third and final written reprimand. 'I think of it as the cardinal rule. We *never* say no.'

*

I have to say that it was more of a relief than anything to be terminated before the arrival on board of the no-doubt lovely and erudite and uncreasable Mrs Short. And after so long aboard an American cruise ship, it was no small consolation that by the time my reprimands had been collated and the paperwork for my dismissal finalised, the ship had sailed into the sisterly waters of Canada.

'Go on then,' said Beth in our cabin on my last morning, handing me the last tissue from the box and wiping her nose with the back of her hand. 'Get out of here.'

I handed in my uniform, smiled insincerely at Natarsha, and clodded down the ship's gangway in my dear old Doc Martens, onto a wharf in a city half-rimmed by mountains.

I felt heavy, and not only because of the weight of the two suitcases I carried. But I tried to buoy myself with the knowledge that this city was the one I would most probably have chosen, if I'd had to choose a city in which to be cast out. It was, after all, the city within whose credibly ramshackle arts precinct was my favourite tearoom in the world.

The Junction Tearoom was a converted house: the kind of grand old home that would once have had lawns and a tennis court and a commanding view of its surrounds, but was now squeezed tight into a corner block by the encroachment of urban clutter. Its wide and rickety verandas were glassed in and filled with rattan chairs and small, unsteady tables, each with a pile of assorted secondhand books, their topics alternately banal and arcane. But it was within the former bedrooms and sitting rooms and drawing rooms of the old house that the real magic of the Junction resided, since each of these rooms was lined with shelves, and all of these shelves were filled with teacups.

To wander through the house was to chart the modern history of the teacup. Represented were all the great potteries, and the lesser ones too, all the famous patterns, and many of the forgotten as well. There were ladies' cups and children's cups, Victorian cups and art deco cups, serious cups and silly cups. And not one of them was behind glass. They were there to be used. At the Junction, you see, you not only ordered tea, but a teacup too. Each was assigned a number, and had tucked into its saucer a small card detailing its provenance. Predictably, there were Junction devotees whose mission it was to have tea from each and every cup in the collection.

I arrived there late in the morning and chose a table whose pile of books was topped by a yellow-jacketed tome titled *British Poultry Standards*. And although I walked through all of the interior rooms and looked at the hundreds of cups I could choose from, and considered seriously a gold-lined Aynsley with burnished fruit, a Blue Paragon with roses and a Womble cup depicting four of the little scavengers paddling a bathtub, the cup I really wanted was one that I had drunk from before. I knew that I should try something different, but I was feeling low, and in need of comfort, and it was no time to be stern with myself. So I asked for the Red Domino (Midwinter Pottery, 1953, designer Jessie Tait), a good-sized white cup with a red rim that was trimmed with small white dots, and it was brought to my table, along with a plain white teapot and milk jug, by a waiter with a black apron strung tightly across his narrow hips.

Outside it was raining, and although I was not exactly cold, I could still have done with a quilt to pop over my knees, or a hot-water bottle to hold against my chest. I poured my tea and drifted into the clear circle of thinking space that seemed to open up around it. Well, I thought, I had excelled myself this time. Within a matter of days I had bruised my heart and lost my job, however unlovely the job. Was this how it was to be for me? Instead of learning to make fewer mistakes, I would simply rack them up more swiftly?

These were the questions I was asking of myself as I looked out through the drizzling window, and saw somebody that I did not expect to see. It was her. Surely. She was on the wrong continent, of course. And she did not appear to have aged a day in the ten years since I'd seen her last, on a train chuffing through the English countryside. But it had to be her. She was wearing the very same polka-dot dress with the flopping polka-dot bow at its throat, and the same neat little black shoes with their laces and high heels. She carried the same umbrella, but it was opened this time, and she held it steadily above her head as she stood on the corner across the street from the tearoom, looking directly at me.

Raindrops bounced on her polka-dot canopy and the traffic lights changed. And changed again. And then one more time. But she simply stood there, half-smiling at me, until — at last — I understood. That she had been there at every crucial junction, in one guise or another. She was there, that night in the Hyphen-Wilson's boatshed, pinned to the wall as Miss August, wearing nothing more than the pants of a polka-dot bikini. She was at the hospital on the night I had six stitches between my eyes, her long blonde hair held back with a polka-dot bandana while she asked me questions and allowed me to tell myself the truth. She was the smut-cheeked child with the Christmas wreath, and the hand in the spotted glove that I had noticed hovering protectively at the edge of one of the photographs taken on the day of my christening. She was what I had been reaching for when I had chosen, on this very day, the dot-rimmed cup that I now held in my hand.

I smiled at her across the shallow river of the wet road. And she smiled back, and lifted one hand to wave: the kind of wave in which the four fingers move as they would in a quick scale of as many piano keys. She stepped off the kerb then, and, without waiting for the lights to change, crossed the road. She entered the tearoom and the chime-bells of the door continued to tinkle while she shook the raindrops off her umbrella, collapsed and furled it. For just a moment, I doubted myself. Perhaps she would simply sit down at any one of the empty tables and order a cup of tea. But no. She took a seat at my table, and as she did so the waiter set down in front of her a cup that was black with white polka-dots, resting in a saucer that was white with black. Of course.

'I came to tell you something,' she said, pouring milk, and then tea, from my jug and my teapot, into her cup.

'Tell me something?'

'Mmmmm,' she said. 'Isn't it wonderful when the first sip

of tea is precisely the right temperature? One of the great pleasures in life, in my book.'

'You were saying? That you came to tell me something?'

'Oh yes,' she said, her smile revealing some flecks of cerise lipstick on her front teeth. She sipped her tea again.

'What did you come to tell me?' I asked, trying to keep my impatience in check.

She took another sip and inclined her head towards me.

'That your laces are undone, dear,' she said softly.

My laces? I looked down at my boots.

'And in here, too, dear,' she said, tapping with skewed and wrinkled fingers at the centre of her polka-dot chest.

I looked inward at my heart. And indeed, there too, the criss-cross corsetry was slackened and gaping. I was all undone. Potentially, I could spill. Or tangle. And so I began to tug at my own heartstrings, pulling them up tight until there was just the right amount of tension at each criss and each cross. Then I bent down to my boots and laced them firmly too, first the left, then the right, finishing off on each side with a surgeon's shoelace knot.

But when I looked up from my boots, eager to ask who, where, when, why…she was gone.

She was no longer in the tearoom, and she was not anywhere to be seen in the street. The waiter shrugged in answer to my searching face. She had simply vanished, leaving her polka-dot cup on the table, half full of milky tea. I put my hand on the side of her cup and felt both the warmth of it, and the warmth of the knowledge that she was out there. Somewhere.

My heart swelled gently within the safe net of its lacing, and my toes flexed inside their casing of cherry-red leather. In a moment, I would take a bold and good-sized step, out into the woods again. But first, I would finish my tea.

A NOTE ON SOURCES

The line from Christopher Hampton's play *Les Liaisons dangereuses* that appears on p. 8 is reproduced with permission from publisher Faber and Faber Ltd. Information contained in 'A Word from Rosie Little On Penises', pp. 11–13, was drawn from a range of sources including *Ever Since Adam and Eve: The Evolution of Human Sexuality*, by Roger Short and Malcolm Potts, and *The Penis Book*, by Joseph Cohen. The Elephant Information Repository referred to in 'Elephantiasis' can be found online at elephant.elepost.com. My thanks to Jessica Dietrich from the University of Tasmania and Judith Hallett from the University of Maryland for verifying the Latin translation of *Twinkle Twinkle Little Star* on p. 193.

ACKNOWLEDGMENTS

For being Rosie's perfect reader and first editor: Anica Boulanger-Mashberg.

For laughs, and for listening and never seeming to mind: Heather Brown.

For angelic guidance (and laughs too): Heather Rose.

For backwards spelling lessons: Brother Brian Godfrey.

For advice and assistance: Alan Champion, Maeve Arwel, Robyn and Adrian Colman, Geoffrey Kirkland, Graeme Riddoch, Andrew Sant, Elle Leane and Joanna Longbottom.

For wit, wisdom, friendship and allowing the occasional petty theft: Nelli Noakes, Jane Hutchinson, Kate Mooney, Lou Braithwaite, Mona Blackfish, Claire Konkes, Anna Johnston, Lisa Fletcher, Andrea Crompton, Katherine 'Fuzzle' Legg, Rachael Treasure, Carol Altmann, Joanna Richardson, Yvette Blackwood, the Curry Girls, the CRAFT sisterhood and honorary girlfriend Sister Peter Sharp.

For various aquiline noses: my colleagues at the University of Tasmania.

For energy: my students at the University of Tasmania.

For 'supervising': Richard Rossiter and Barbara Mobbs.

For making Rosie real: Annette Barlow, Christa Munns,

Ali Lavau, Andrew Hawkins and all at Allen & Unwin.

For being the family of a writer, with all that it entails: Jenny and Peter Wood, John Godfrey, Axel Rooney and the Divine Miss X.

ABOUT THE AUTHOR

Danielle Wood's first novel, *The Alphabet of Light and Dark*, won several literary awards and two of the stories from *Rosie Little's Cautionary Tales for Girls* were published in the *Best Australian Stories* anthology series. A former journalist, she teaches writing at the University of Tasmania. She is currently at work on her third novel, *Of a Feather*.